DEDICATION

This book is dedicated to the memory of my father Robert Cundiff who was taken from our family too early in 1983.

The Cold November Son

Kjelden Cundiff

Copyright © 2010 Kjelden Cundiff
All rights reserved.
ISBN: 1456427326
ISBN-13: 9781456427320

CONTENTS

    Acknowledgments   i

1	Summer Break	Pg 3
2	A Family Tradition	Pg 9
3	Namesake	Pg 12
4	A Passage Through Time	Pg 23
5	Jensen's Hardware	Pg 28
6	Avery	Pg 35
7	Fourteen Candles	Pg 41
8	The Apprentice	Pg 46
9	The Rage of Easy	Pg 54
10	Dinner Conversation	Pg 67
11	More Human Than We Know	Pg 72
12	Brimstone and Lies	Pg 81
13	Mind Over Matter	Pg 89
14	A Secret No More	Pg 91
15	Learning to Lie	Pg 99
16	Hypocrisy	Pg 102
17	A Broken Glass	Pg 115
18	Cold as a January Storm	Pg 121
19	A Day at the Lake	Pg 126
20	Listen to your Heart	Pg 130
21	Dreams of Maples	Pg 150
22	Snowflakes	Pg 156
23	Quiet Ride	Pg 159
24	Remnants of a Harvest	Pg 165
25	It's Time	Pg 170
26	The Cold November Son	Pg 176

ACKNOWLEDGMENTS

Thank you to my wife Lisa for her endless support of my passion for writing and encouragement to pursue my dream.

Chapter 1

There are moments that define our lives, landmark events that are forever frozen in our minds and mark the beginning of a passage from one stage of our lives into another.

In the summer of 1983, I had one of those moments. It thrust me forward, made me more mature, and brought me closer to manhood than I had ever been before.

That summer started innocently enough. The memory of that first day of summer break is still emblazoned like a tattoo on my memory, as brilliantly colored now as when it was happening.

A bookmark etched so deeply into my mind that it will never be forgotten by me. A trail of dust rose up from behind the tires of my father's 1953 GMC pickup. It had been a dry spring and it didn't take much to stir the dust loose from the rock and gravel packed country roads.

My father's truck was a golden bronze color topped with a milky white cab.

The pickup's exterior was charming and had a classic look to it with its bulky rounded fenders and menacingly large chrome front bumper.

The paint had faded through the years and rocks from the many unpaved roads it had traversed had left their marks as they were tossed into the air by the large knobby tires and shot back into the truck, chipping away at the golden bronze finish. Through my eyes though there was something about my father's truck that held a beauty that extended far beneath the golden colored layers of paint that covered the heavy steel fenders. The truck from my perspective was really a giant steel and glass extension of my father's personality. It was symbolic of both his toughness and his loyalty. That pickup had never failed my father and his loyalty to it was equal. It was his work companion and his confidant. I was certain that he had held many conversations in the cab of that pickup with no one else sitting inside.

That truck was an inanimate object yet it had taken on an almost human persona.

I sat on the ripped green vinyl seat of an old kitchen chair suspended over a set of four skinny chrome legs. The chair had been moved one step closer to the trash pile. It had been brought from the kitchen inside of the house to the wooden porch outside. It served me well here on the weather beaten planks of the wooden porch that ran the length of the front side of our house.

The distant noise of the vehicle that was approaching lifted my attention from the book I was reading. I lowered my head so I could see underneath the large leafy maple tree that flourished along the side of our driveway. The maple tree had started as a mere sapling and a memorial to my late uncle Tommy. It now reached skyward to the place where my uncle always felt most comfortable.

I spotted a vehicle traveling on the country road that connected our driveway to County Road 86, a lightly traveled road. It was my father's truck. I recognized it in the distance driving in my direction.

My father arrived home early that first day of summer break. Arriving home early was an unusual occurrence. It was rare for him to come home in the middle of the day unless an outdoor work project had been cut short by bad weather. On a sun washed day like today, he worked from sunrise to nightfall and right now the sun was nowhere near the western horizon.

My father was a large man in stature. He stood just over six feet four inches tall and weighed in at well over two hundred and forty pounds. His hands were callused and scarred from a lifetime of hard work as a carpenter and a construction laborer.

The veins in his hands were easily visible through his tan leathery skin. They were thick and pressed outward. The veins formed a set of greenish blue ridges that ran like a spider's web from his forearms to his knuckles.

His hair was thick and black. He wore it short and combed back with the help of some Brylcream. His hairstyle was the same fashion that he had worn it for as long as I could tell. I say that because of the many times that I had looked through my grandparent's family photo album. Inside there were pictures of my dad that spanned from his teenage years all the way up to his wedding day. Those pictures represented over two decades of time and his appearance was essentially the same now as it was then.

My father was slightly heavier now than he appeared in those photographs of him as a younger man but that was the only noticeable difference. His face was a little rounder than before but other than the change in his weight, which he had gained over the years, he was essentially the same gentle giant he had always been.

He had a strong jaw line that jutted forward and in the middle of his chin there was a distinct dimple that made a deep indentation.

Time had aged my father in some ways that were not so different from the way it had aged his 1953 GMC pickup. Dad was slightly worn but beneath the scarred exterior of his body there remained a skeletal frame strung together by muscles and tendons that was still as strong and sturdy as it had ever been.

His broad shoulders emerged first from the cab of the truck filling the frame where the door hung on its hinges.

"Come here for a second I want to show you something."

His voice cut like a freshly sharpened scythe through the humid sunshine as a warm summer breeze tried in futility to push the moistened air off the front porch of our house.

Seeing my father so early in the day was a welcome interruption even though I was deeply engrossed in reading the latest Doc Savage novel I had purchased.

I loved to read and Doc Savage had become my most recent obsession. Used paperbacks were only twenty-five cents each at the bookstore, the same price as a game of pinball but a book could entertain me all weekend.

The fantastic adventures of the muscle bound Doc Savage offered an escape from the rather bland world I lived in, a stark contrast to the flat rolling plains of Eastern South Dakota

I stood up and bounced down the four wooden steps barefooted to the cement sidewalk. I followed closely behind my father as he circled around the truck to the passenger door. His hands were covered in a thin layer of dust. A small dribble of perspiration slowly carved a trail through the dusty coating on his skin until it reached the edge of his hand where it fell harmlessly to the dirt below.

Dad squeezed the chrome button inward on the passenger side door handle popping open the latch that held it shut. The door creaked on its hinges as he swung it open.

He stepped up on the running board and reached over the bench seat. When he moved back from inside of the pickup, he was holding a long beige gun case.

The gun case was dirty and the handle was broken. It had been sloppily repaired with the help of some duct tape.

He sat the gun case on the hood of the pickup, slowly backed away from it smiling proudly and then looked in my direction awaiting a response. A few seconds passed when he could no longer contain his excitement.

"Well, open it," he exclaimed eagerly.

I was somewhat stunned by the whole event that was taking place in front of me and stood with my fingers in the novel carefully marking the page where I had stopped reading. I folded over the corner of the page I had finished reading, and sat the book on the running board of the truck.

I anxiously stepped forward to unzip the tattered gun case. My interest in the book had been quickly replaced by the mystery of what lay inside of brown and beige gun case.

I tugged on the zipper of the gun case peeling it open from one end to the other. I took my hands and gently lifted the top half of the gun case and laid it above the bottom half. Lying there on a quilted green and blue plaid cloth lining was a shotgun with a dark brown stock and a charcoal colored barrel.

"Go ahead and see how that fits you", my father chirped excitedly.

See how that fits you, as if I were trying on a new jacket or a pair of blue jeans. This was a far cry from any ordinary piece of clothing. This was a shotgun! I knew how important it was to be able to hold a shotgun firmly so that I could be in control while shooting with it.

"It's for me?"

"It's a Browning twenty gauge. You're gonna be fourteen in a few days and we can use another sharpshooter this fall."

I rested the gunstock against my right shoulder and followed a couple of blackbirds with it as they flew across the blue canvas of the cloudless sky pretending to shoot them. The shotgun fit me perfectly but even if it hadn't I would have lied and said it did.

This was an enormous moment for me. Now I could go pheasant hunting with my uncles Art and Earl and my father on those crisp South Dakota fall mornings. Unofficially, I was finally one of them, the men. For me, that moment marked one critical step toward manhood; one of many that I was about to take that summer.

Chapter 2

My adrenalin swirled inside of me as I was overwhelmed with excitement. For the last several hunting seasons we had talked about the time when I would be carrying my own gun on a hunting trip. I had been patiently waiting for that day when I would no longer just serve as a two-legged hunting dog. Until now my role had always been to walk the cornfields and flush the pheasants up from the cover of the muddy cornrows toward my father and my uncles as they waited to gun them down as they took flight.

When I was younger, I didn't care that I wasn't carrying a shotgun while on our hunting trips. Just being out there with the men of the family was satisfying enough for me. After all, I was still there side by side with my father. I felt like I was trapped inside the body of an eight-year old as I waited patiently to become a man.

Even when I wasn't carrying a shotgun my dad made me feel important during our outings. As he explained to me, I was the one who scared the pheasants out into the open where they could be seen. Dad said that without me chasing the birds from the cover of the brush there would be nothing for my uncles or him to shoot at.

My father and his brothers were what the locals called "ringers". Each was an excellent marksman. Years earlier when they were my age they had been the boys who acted as the bird dogs that walked the fields and herded the pheasants toward their own father and uncles, now my two cousins and I had taken on that role.

My two cousins were named Joey and Junior. My cousin Joey was a chubby kid and two years younger than I was. He went along on the hunting trips because he was expected to, not because of the excitement or the desire to hunt. While I cherished the moment, Joey was simply fulfilling his father's expectations. He lacked the physical toughness of his older brother Junior. Joey complained about everything from how cold it was to how long the walks through the muddy fields were.

My cousin Junior on the other hand was as excited as I was about the autumn ritual. He was a big kid, about my age, but several inches taller than me and much stronger. The frame of his body clearly resembled the same large frame as that of my uncle Earl and my father. Junior was tall, broad shouldered and strong.

Both Junior and I chattered up a storm riding in the truck on the way to the hunt. Once we were on our way to a hunting trip, we never gave a second thought to the cold damp autumn weather. That was how I could tell the difference between Joey's desire to go on the hunting trips and the interest that Junior and I had. Joey couldn't wait for the day to end so he could go home and get out of the inclement weather while Junior and would have gladly stayed outside long after our parents were exhausted or had reached their limit of birds for the day.

My cousins and I weren't only out in the fields during pheasant season. We were also out there in the middle of the summer working. Both my cousins and I had walked the soybean fields together during the summer, not to chase out pheasants but rather to pull weeds.

Those long days of walking the soybean fields were dreaded by each of us. It was exhausting work sprinkled with a touch of humidity and flying insects. Those summer days were nothing like the days we spent in the corn fields and soybean fields in the fall. During the fall it was no longer work but rather the men of the family carrying on a longtime tradition of hunting pheasants.

Both occasions served as times that I bonded with my cousins, under the hot and humid summer sun while we blistered our hands pulling milkweed, thistle and wild grass and on those crisp fall hunting trips when our foggy breath hung in the air with each frozen exhalation.

Chapter 3

My father left the family farm shortly after graduating from high school and enlisted in the army. Uncle Art and uncle Earl stayed behind and continued working the land and raising the livestock. His kid brother Tommy was less passionate about working the land than his older brothers but that didn't keep him from helping in his own way. He started his own business where he not only worked on the family farm but on farms all over the county.

Once my father found a path that led him away from the farm, he eagerly followed it. He admired his father and brothers for their love of farming but he wanted to see what else was out there in that mysterious place we call the world. Up until the time that he left the farm my father's world had only extended several miles from where he had grown up.

If at the end of my father's journey he had discovered nothing else that satisfied him more than farming did then he would gladly be welcomed back home with open arms. However, he first had to satisfy the never-ending internal curiosity that burned inside of him since he was a teenager.

As it turned out my father never returned home to work on the farm again. After my father enlisted in the army he was a soldier for four years and during that time he did a tour of duty in Vietnam. That wasn't the destination he had dreamed of when he fantasized of seeing the world but the experience did help to make him more mature and gave him a perspective on life that he might not have otherwise received. When he finally returned stateside he was stationed in New York and that's where he met my mother.

My mom was working as a hostess at her parent's restaurant, a favorite watering hole for the enlisted men that were stationed nearby. She was only eighteen but she was breathtakingly beautiful and caught my father's eye the first time he stepped through the door of her family's restaurant.

As he tells the story she was standing just inside of the entrance of the restaurant cradling a stack of menus and looking downward. My father was caught staring at her when she unexpectedly raised her head to look around.

It was love at first sight for both of them. Thousands of other servicemen had entered her parent's restaurant before my father but this time the man in the neatly pressed uniform caught my mother's attention. Dad was both handsome and imposing. His presence when he entered a room always seemed to gather attention. It was something about his size, his posture and the gentle smile that he brought with him wherever he went. Some people just have a charisma and that intangible something that draws the eyes of others to them.

His presence hadn't escaped my mother's watchful eye as she seated his buddies and him in a corner booth. Whether it was on purpose or not she made sure that their table left a clear and unimpaired visual path to her hostess stand.

Throughout that night my mother and father shared several innocent yet flirtatious glances. Dad was able to hold his stare longer than my mother was. If he gazed long enough she would end up modestly turning her face in the other direction.

Dad says he finished eating and then waited for an opportunity when there weren't any customers waiting to be seated by my mother, the hostess. When the opportunity finally arrived, my father quickly walked up, introduced himself, and asked my mother if she would like to join him for dinner that Saturday night. My grandfather upon seeing my father and his daughter engaged in a giggling conversation wasted no time in making his way over to them. Grandpa introduced himself and then held a brief interrogation of my father to find out who this stranger was that was so clearly enamored with his teenage daughter.

My father having several years of army training engrained in him politely asked her father if he would allow his daughter to join him for a dinner date.

My grandfather must have been impressed with my father's manners and respectful nature, because he let down his normally overprotective nature and permitted my mother go on a date. From that point forward things moved quickly between my mother and father but for two very different reasons. Dad was love struck and infatuated with my mother's beauty. Mom was attracted as well but not just to my father's appearance but also with the opportunity to escape the tight clutch of her parent's smothering arms.

My mother was mature beyond her eighteen years when my father met her and she was anxious to make a life for herself away from her parents. She was rarely out of their view and found them to be both controlling and overly religious. What she desired as life's pleasures her parents equated to be sin. Their desire to shelter her backfired, drove her to become an independent young woman, and sent her seeking for a way to flee their scrutiny.

A whirlwind courtship followed and a year later upon my father's honorable discharge from the army they married and moved to the small town of Lake Mills, South Dakota. My mom suddenly found herself a comfortable fifteen hundred miles or so out of her parents reach. Two short years after my parents moved to the town of Lake Mills I was born, their first and only child.

My father didn't return to farming upon leaving the army. Instead, he launched his own construction business in Lake Mills. He took whatever work he could find whether it was painting houses or mending fences. Financially it was a struggle, which would be a challenge for any set of newlyweds rearing a newborn but it was especially challenging for my mother whose parents had never left her wanting for any material thing that she ever desired.

Dad claims that my mother accepted the changes both in geography and lifestyle and together somehow they toughed it out during those early years of marriage.

Finding work was slow early on and my father never turned down a job. As long as he was allowed to be his own boss he was satisfied. He was determined to control his own destiny. He could never underscore that point to me enough, about his desire to control his own destiny. That concept of being independent and having the ability to shape his own future was extremely important to my father.

Lake Mills was larger than his hometown of Cedar Springs, South Dakota. The local economy was not solely dependent on agriculture, which was also a reason why my parents settled where they did.

Lake Mills was a growing city with a movie theater, a shopping mall and a nearby lake, which was a gathering spot for the locals in the summer. Each of those amenities helped my mother transition from the fast pace of New York to the laid back tempo of the Midwest. However, even though Lake Mills was thriving, it was in many ways still a typical small Midwestern town; with a cobblestone Main Street, modest homes and elm treed boulevards. It was a working class community that kept intact a value system that some larger cities were beginning to abandon. It was geographically far enough away from my mother's family, which allowed her to spread her wings and grow.

To understand my father's strong desire to leave the family business of agriculture you had to look at the occupation of being a farmer through his eyes. To my father farming had always been an exercise in faith, luck and hard work. He had seen his parents struggle through droughts; hail storms and poor market prices. He had heard the stories of The Great Depression. He wanted no part of the insecure feeling that he watched his father wash away with ice-cold bottles of beer when thunderheads began forming in the western skies.

Dad blamed farming on his father's premature death. Months worth of hard work and twelve-hour days were always just one summer storm away from being lost forever. Grain prices remained stagnant while inflation, fuel prices, and world politics put a constant strain on American agriculture and the family farm.

The economics of farming were a preoccupation that constantly weighed on his own father's mind. Often times the worries were so great it would leave my grandfather restless and nursing a cold bottle of whatever beer was on sale that week at the local tavern. Often times my grandfather could be found sitting at the kitchen table in the hours between midnight and five in the morning. Those beers were nothing more than cold twelve-ounce liquid tranquilizers. Unfortunately, their temporary relief couldn't change the path of an impending storm and they couldn't bring the much-needed rain when the soil became lighter than the air that blew across it.

Dad's memories of the untold number of sleepless nights that he witnessed my grandfather endure was a huge influence on my father's desire to control his financial destiny.

That wish along with two devastating tragedies that happened shortly before I was born changed my father's outlook on life forever.

I had heard the story of my namesake, my father's brother Tommy, many times. I had seen Uncle Tommy's picture at the family farm when my grandmother still lived there. My grandmother kept his picture on her nightstand next to a tarnished silver cross and a rosary. The picture was of my uncle Tommy standing next to his pride and joy, his crop duster.

My grandmother never fully recovered from the loss of her youngest son Tommy. She would hold his picture in her left hand and have the rosary and silver cross necklace woven between the fingers on her right hand. Sometimes she sobbed outwardly and sometimes the only thing that came from her eyes was the lonely stare of an aged mother who was mourning the premature death of a child. I can still hear the echoes of my grandmother's voice calling to me to her room when we would visit.

"Tommy, come here."

I'm not sure why but I was afraid of her bedroom. Something about her bedroom was eerie to me with its thick dark fabric draperies and cold wooden plank floor. Before going into her bedroom I would calm my fears with a few deep breaths. Then after I was relaxed I would obediently walk inside angling slowly toward her large iron bed frame.

"Always be a good boy Tommy and do what papa tells you to do."

Grandma spoke with a thick accent, a leftover from her childhood when she only spoke Danish until the age of five.

"It's not right when a mama loses her baby. I told him to be careful but God called him home anyway. Listen to papa. Papa will always know what is best."

My grandmother had deep lines in her face. The sun, stress and pain from the loss of her child had each taken a toll and left a mark on her leathery skin.

Most of the memories I have of my grandmother took place in her bedroom. She spent a large portion of the day lying in her bed, sometimes sleeping and sometimes reading. I tried my best to give her comfort at her bedside. She would grip me and pull me forward with her bony hands. Her arms shook as she tried to raise herself up in her bed. I reached down and pulled her up by lifting her from under her arms around her ribcage. Once she was elevated I sat her up by propping her tiny body against a stack of pillows.

On one of my last visits to my grandmother while she was still alive I was sitting on the side of her bed. On that day she was clutching at me and she was exceptionally quiet. She stared up at my face to an area over my shoulder on the wall behind me. I turned my head expecting to see a bug or shadow but there was nothing there except for the dark wallpapered wall.

My grandmother's eyelids closed shut producing a tiny stream of tears. The tears ran along her nose and then followed the path of the wrinkles that were etched so deeply into her face. The wrinkles ran sharply from her cheekbones to the corners of her mouth. She used those tears to moisten her lips with her tongue.

My grandmother's mouth was hollow and sunken when she had her dentures out. Her eyes were also sunken and filled with sadness and grief.

She sat the picture of my uncle Tommy back on the nightstand and gently stroked the side of my face with her right palm. She held the cold chain of the rosary pressed against my skin until her voice fell silent and only her eyes were left to speak to me.

I stared into her faded blue pupils as if I were looking through a tunnel. I imagined that the tunnel led to an empty spot somewhere squarely at the center of her soul. That voided area would represent the part of her that had once been filled by the life of her youngest child, my uncle Tommy.

I stood there quietly waiting for her to drift off to sleep. I leaned my thighs against the mattress of her bed to support my tired legs. Once she had fallen asleep, I carefully released my hand from her grip and laid her hand down on the mattress next to her.

I then left the room by carefully stepping on the spots of the wood floor where I knew it was less likely to make a creaking sound. I had been in and out of her bedroom so many times that I had memorized which planks to avoid while tiptoeing so I could make as little noise as possible.

Uncle Tommy's death had an impact on the entire family, not just my grandmother. Not only had his unexpected death changed my grandmother forever but it stung my father extremely hard as well. The hurt from his premature death however did not impact my dad nearly as harshly as his own father's death.

There were some very good reasons for this, primarily because my uncle Tommy had been doing what he loved when he died. The entire family agreed on this. Uncle Tommy was flying his plane, spraying for insects, and probably pretending that he was piloting a commercial airliner thirty thousand feet above the ground when life became death just a few moments later.

Flying a crop duster is a dangerous occupation. The pilots have to fly very low and maneuver the small fragile planes with precision, perfect timing and delicate turns. Death is a well-known occupational hazard for the people who choose to fly these planes but the freedom of flight and the exhilaration of the ride are irresistible for an adrenalin junkie.

Uncle Tommy had flown hundreds of times but on his final flight, his plane hit the top of a tree with the tip of its wing turning his crop duster sideways and driving it downward and into the ground. That grove of trees that he had avoided a hundred times before appeared too quickly on that day.

It was death on impact with no chance to react and little chance to survive. Nevertheless, the family except for my grandmother mourned his death as a triumph. He died courageously living out his dream and knowing the risks that were involved.

My father said it had always been my uncle's dream since they were children to fly airplanes. He had wanted to do nothing else since the moment he saw a crop duster spinning through the sky for the first time. Something inside of my uncle Tommy from that moment forward compelled him to pursue his dream of flying. Maybe it was the danger of the flights or possibly it was his fascination he felt as he floated over the black and green fields. Perhaps as my father believed, it was my uncle's divine fate. An unforeseeable misfortune sent as a message from God so that the people closest to him would pursue their own dreams and never take a day of life for granted again.

Three months before my uncle's death my father's family had endured another loss when my grandfather passed away. My grandfather's demise was much different however from my uncle Tommy's untimely passing.

Grandpa's death was a slow, painful and inescapable decline. There was nothing quick and painless about his death. In fact, his death was so foreshadowed that the family had mourned for several months before his final desperate gasp for air, a sound that I later came to know as "the death rattle".

My grandfather suffered with stomach cancer. A long slow downward spiral followed his diagnosis. While my uncle Tommy had less than two seconds before impact to contemplate his fate, my grandfather had eight months to consider the hereafter and to say his goodbyes.

In the end, my grandfather spent the last several weeks of his life slowly wasting away in a bed. Finally, when his suffering became too unbearable for the family to witness he was brought to the county hospital where he languished for another week in a near coma, unable to eat or to take care of himself.

He died a mere shadow of the once strong and formidable farmer that he had always been. He had suffered extreme weight loss, muscle atrophy, but most importantly, a loss of his dignity and independence.

Grandpa was harvesting one of the best wheat crops his farm had ever yielded the fall he learned of his illness. Stress, smoking and a penchant for Grain Belt beer on those humid summer days and those freezing winter nights may have contributed to his early departure but no doctor could say for sure what caused him to get cancer.

It was a devastating time for my father, a man trying to make a fresh start with a beautiful new bride. First his father, and then his youngest brother, both taken away from him in two very different ways a mere three months apart.

His younger brother strong, healthy and feeling the exhilaration of flight when his life turned to death and his father crippled, bedridden and praying for a merciful end to his suffering when he finally drew in one final breath.

Both of these deaths sent ripples of emotions smashing their way through the guts of my father. The deaths caused two very different sets of emotions, each a result of the manners in which his brother and father had passed away.

Tommy would forever be revered for pursuing his dream of flight and dying while doing what he loved. Life had never cheated my uncle out of anything. He had lived his short life with passion and pleasure right up to the moment of impact.

On the other hand, my grandfather had used alcohol and cigarettes to cope with the daily stresses of farming for decades. Grandpa loved farming but my father never believed that he had died doing what he loved. He believed my grandfather had fallen ill doing what he loved. To my father there was a distinct difference between dying while doing something you love and falling ill while doing a job. My grandfather had spent eight painful months suffering through the effects of the cancer as it ate its way through his body but he had spent years leading up to that moment in a constant state of anxiety, worrying about what the next day would bring.

I never understood the importance or connection of these two tragic events that preceded my own birth until much later, when life would deal me my own unexpected tragedy. My father put it into terms that were unmistakably clear. The importance of pursuing your dreams and dying on your own terms should always be at the forefront of one's mind. Also, one should never make the mistake of overlooking today because of worries about a storm that may be lurking on the horizon.

That was the lesson learned by my father from these two separate yet entangled misfortunes. It was a lesson he was going to make sure that I would discover as well. My father and I had conversations about my uncle and grandfather many, many times. I think partly to keep their memories alive but mostly so that I would have a better understanding of how to see the world through my father's eyes.

That is why he had named me after his younger brother, a man he always held in the highest regard. It is also the reason that he had planted a tree as a living memorial to my uncle Tommy just in front of our house. That tree was planted so that we would never forget the lessons learned from my uncle's premature demise.

That innocent looking tree was the same kind of tree that my uncle's crop-duster had become entangled in.

The maple tree along our driveway was layered with symbolism. It represented life and the changing of the seasons. It represented the memory of a lost sibling and a man who was always growing and reaching new heights. And it represented beauty as only a maple tree can in the fall when its' leaves turn into a sea of orange and red foliage.

Uncle Tommy had lived, I mean really lived every moment of his life. Dad said my name was in part a tribute to his brother's life but it was also given in hopes that I would embrace that same attitude that Tommy had embraced. The philosophy of living for the moment and taking nothing for granted.

With both tragedies still vivid memories it was difficult for my father to choose to not carry on the family legacy and manage the farm with his remaining brothers. He loved the farm but not enough to forfeit his dreams. He felt pressure to take on the responsibilities that his brother and father had left behind but he overcame the guilt and feeling of obligation and pursued his own dream.

Dad wanted a better life for his family, more stability, and most importantly control of his own destiny. It turns out that everything he wanted would be far more elusive than one of those brilliantly colored pheasants that we chased on the weekends through muddy fields and through groves of trees on foggy fall days under the cold November sun.

Chapter 4

I returned the shotgun to the case and zipped it shut.
"Where is your mother?" Dad inquired.
"Church."
My mom had always been religious but she had recently become more devout. She was starting to call herself a "born again Christian". She was spending more time at the local Pentecostal church and less and less time at home. She was slowly returning to the life she had so eagerly escaped some sixteen years earlier. Prayer meetings, fundraisers and bible study groups dominated her schedule. It was hard for my father to criticize my mother for being away from home when she was becoming more in touch with her own spirituality but I could see the displeasure on his face growing over these past few months.
"I guess that means you and I get to go out and test your new gun."
"Really?"
I could hardly contain my excitement. I had been to the firing range many times with my father but always as a guest and never as a participant.
"You've got four months before pheasant season starts. I want you to show up your cousin Junior out there."

There had always been a friendly competition between my father and my uncles. They got a kick out of pitting their sons' outdoor skills against each other. Cousin Joey being younger was at a disadvantage. He would not be carrying a gun this fall but I knew that Junior would be and I was determined to be a better shot than he was.

"I'm going to run in and wash up", I said excitedly.

"No need to clean up, throw on some jeans and a tee shirt and we'll hit the road before your mother gets home."

I could read between the lines. My mother did not care for the idea of hunting. Unlike my father, she hadn't grown up on a farm. She was the product of a conservative religious family. She had grown up in New York City, which did not embrace the same cultural ideals as the people who populated this rural area of eastern South Dakota.

Mom accepted soldiers and understood their needs for guns but to her hunting wild game was archaic, cruel and an unnecessary sport. She would never embrace hunting but she tolerated it nonetheless much like my father tolerated the inordinate amount of time she spent attending church, searching for some elusive internal happiness.

My mother also knew how much my dad looked forward to each fall when he could go back to the family farm and spend Saturday and Sunday afternoon with his brothers. Those weekend hunting trips were like traveling through a time machine for him.

My grandparents' family farmhouse although abandoned now served as a doorway to the past for my father. Its interior was rotting from the many change of seasons it had endured and also from a chronically leaky roof. The farmhouse no longer sheltered any humans but rather housed several families of mice.

The interior was still decorated the same as it had been when my father was my age. The wallpaper still hugged the walls of the living room and kitchen. It was pink and white striped with a faint floral pattern running through the vertical stripes in it. The thick white baseboards that connected the wallpaper to the dried and cracked linoleum floor still framed the wall.

The crown molding was now warped and peeling and the ceilings were sagging where the rain had leaked in leaving a series of yellowish brown circles. The stains themselves were layered with even newer stains from the water that had soaked and dried over the years. They resembled the rings on the stump of a freshly cut tree trunk. The faded black pot bellied stove still stood where it had sat sixty years earlier, just past the entryway of the kitchen door. On top of the stove stood a round black pipe that carried the smoke through the ceiling and then out to a vent that clung flimsily to the decaying roof.

My grandmother's bed which I had reluctantly visited so many times still sat on the creaky wood plank floor that I had tip toed across so many times. That bedroom now consisted of nothing more than a simple iron bed frame with a box spring and a mattress void of any bedding. The dresser, the nightstands and other furniture had all since been long removed from the farmhouse. Grandma's bed sat alone like an iron island on an oaken ocean.

The house was dilapidated but not to the point where it was unsafe to stand inside. My uncle Art would still live there if it had not been for a tornado that had taken part of the roof with it as it twirled across the prairie. It was a quaint two-story farmhouse but more importantly, it was a symbol of my dad's youth and childhood.

My father never made the ninety-mile trip back to my uncle's homes without visiting the old farmhouse. I watched him closely as we drove up the bumpy gravel driveway. He began smiling five steps before he ever walked through what was left of the front doorway.

That threshold of where the front door had hung now served more like a magical force field to a passageway back in time than it did an entrance to a rotting building.

In my father's mind, he imagined his own father, my grandfather, and his uncles sitting at the kitchen table playing a card game such as cribbage or pinnacle as they did so many nights during his own childhood. Dad envisioned his mother pulling a pot roast out of the oven or perhaps his nasal cavity would capture the sweet and unmistakable smell of her homemade caramel rolls, which would waft up the staircase and greet his brothers and him on those bitterly cold winter mornings signaling that breakfast was ready and waiting to be eaten.

    The joy that grew within my father increased with each step that brought him further inside of the now abandoned house. The memories came rushing towards him faster and faster. They were vivid memories, happy memories of his life as it once had been.

    He did not see the discolored wallpaper that was pulling loose from the living room walls or the stains on the ceilings. Instead he saw his father sitting in a wooden rocking chair on the front porch smoking a pipe and his mother standing at the kitchen counter polishing the silverware that were used on only those very special occasions like Thanksgiving or Easter.

    His mind recalled his brothers sitting on the floor in front of the television wearing toy cowboy hats and gun holsters while they watched westerns.

    It was his favorite part of the ninety-mile journey back home. He never told me that, I just knew. Of course, he loved hunting the pheasants that inhabited the cornfields that his family had farmed for generations but he mostly loved those moments when he could reach into the past by stepping over the decaying threshold of the farmhouse. It was the closest thing he would ever experience to time travel or agelessness.

    There were no home movies of his child hood and only a few still pictures but there was this two-story farmhouse with the wooden front porch, the apple trees and the overgrown yard that had once held so many family picnics.

    The farmhouse was a shrine to time gone by, a symbol of a simpler time. It was a living piece of abstract art. Every passerby who looked at it undoubtedly saw something different. A motorist on the lonely country road might see the decline of the family farm, a once strong symbol of the backbone of America and now a decaying and endangered species. Even I saw the toll that Mother Nature had taken; the missing roof shingles, the broken windowpanes and the shutters with their blistered paint and rotting wood.

It was my father though who saw the farmhouse through the eyes of a teenage boy who grew up in an era that has long since disappeared. He saw the perfectly manicured lawn, the yellow and orange marigold flowers that lined the red brick flowerbed and the white silk curtains that hung in the bay window. He saw the smoke billowing from the red brick chimney and the proud American flag that moved ever so gently in the constant country breeze. It was and would always be his home, his safe haven, and his escape.

Chapter 5

We stopped at the local hardware store to pick up a couple boxes of ammunition. Jensen's Hardware was a family owned business with the owner being an elderly black man who could usually be found running the cash register. Everyone in town knew Mr. Jensen. He was a one of a kind especially in these parts where a black person was as rare as a September snowstorm.

Mr. Jensen was a hard working and fun loving man who took great pride in his business. He had a small store but it had just enough room to keep one of everything.

Classical music was playing through a series of speakers that ran through the ceiling of his store. The interior of the store was an odd mix of wood, steel and Wolfgang Amadeus Mozart.

My father being a carpenter was a frequent customer of Mr. Jensen. There was a new larger and fancier hardware store, which had opened on the outskirts of town but that didn't matter to my father. He held loyalty as one of the most important human qualities a person could possess. Being a small businessman himself, he felt that an alliance amongst all small business owners was for the good of the whole. As long as he needed lumber, nails or in this instance, shotgun shells, there was no question to whom he would give his hard earned money.

As usual, the bell above the door of Jensen's Hardware jingled announcing our entrance. Mr. Jensen's ever-present smile emerged from the office he kept in the back of the store. His posture was a reflection of the lifetime of hard work he had been subjected to, his body slightly tilted to the left and his shoulders slumping and rounded. He had a neatly trimmed gray beard, and salt and pepper tightly curled hair. A toothpick protruded from his glistening white teeth and even though his posture was failing him, he glided along the painted cement floor to the payment counter with the elegance of a ballroom dancer.

"Bob, I see you have an apprentice with you today. Are you spending the summer learning carpentry?"

"No sir."

"This kid's a smart one. I'm thinking doctor or engineer, straight A's second year in a row."

"Is that right? Maybe we got ourselves a future governor standing here among us."

"I want to be a carpenter", I uttered softly.

"A carpenter, just like your old man huh? Well, there ain't nothing' wrong with that. It's a noble profession and if you are as good as your old man is you'll never have trouble finding work."

My dad said doctor but I was sure he meant carpenter. His dream was not any different from my own, but he wanted me to make my own decisions and to be my own man. He never told me that he wished I would be a carpenter like he had chosen to be but I believed that is what he really hoped my future held. I imagined that he fantasized about the two of us working together side by side, just like his father and he had.

"It's his birthday Sunday and I got him a surprise today. Can I get four boxes of twenty gauge shotgun shells?"

"I believe you're in luck."

We followed Mr. Jensen to another counter. Behind it were several rifles and shotguns. He knelt down, took a key ring out of his pocket and unlocked a wire-caged door from behind the counter. He removed four boxes of ammunition and set them on the countertop.

"What else can I get for you fellas today?"

"That's going to do it. We're going to go test his skills against the clay pigeons up at the firing range."

Mr. Jensen knelt back down on the cement floor and locked the cage securely. Dad grabbed the four boxes of shells and followed Mr. Jensen back to the cash register.

"It looks like everyone is taking advantage of the nice weather. I just had me two boys in here getting a couple of new Louisville sluggers so they could head up to the ball fields and have themselves a homerun derby."

"You have yourself a good one Lee and I'll see you next week", my father replied.

"Always a pleasure Bob, as usual always a pleasure."

We left the store and got back into the pickup. Summer break had barely started and I was about to go and fire my shotgun for the first time. My heart began to race. Dad rolled down his window and lit a Pall Mall cigarette. He blew out the match and dropped it into a small crevice in the overflowing ashtray. He kept a pack of Pall Malls in his shirt pocket at all times.

Smoking like hunting was a source of contention between my dad and my mom. To her smoking cigarettes was nothing more than a waste of money. To him it was his only vice. He didn't gamble or drink. He didn't spend money on extravagant items and drove an old pickup, wore blue jeans and pocket tee shirts.

Smoking was his one simple pleasure other than hunting and pheasant season lasted only a few short months each year. Each time he lit a new cigarette he inhaled deeply, treating the taste of the smoke as if he was eating a fine Swiss chocolate. He would then turn his head to the left and exhale the smoke out of the driver's side window. Sometimes he spoke as he exhaled with the smoke punctuating each syllable. Other times the smoke was exhaled through his nose and his mouth simultaneously creating two separate streams of smoke that connected and mixed into a hypnotic smoke like belly dance.

Unlike our house, my dad could smoke in his truck at will. Mom forbade smoking inside our house but she couldn't police him while he was out driving his truck. When he was at home that was a different story and she made the rules. Dad would usually sit on the front porch, get his nicotine fix and put the spent cigarette butts into a rusty old coffee can that was filled with sand.

He had more freedom when he was out on a job site or simply driving along a dusty old gravel road in his truck. I don't mean just freedom to smoke but freedom to relax. I could see it in the way he inhaled and exhaled the smoke. He was savoring the taste. He was relaxed and living in the moment. Smoking a cigarette on the front porch of the house was much more workmanlike. It was hurried, a duty rather than a pleasure.

Unbeknownst to my father I watched him as we drove. As the first cigarette was nearly void of all its tobacco, he reached into his shirt pocket, pulled out the opened pack, gave it a quick jerking motion and extracted a fresh cigarette. This time he did not need a match. He took the finished cigarette from his mouth replacing it with a fresh Pall Mall and then used the cherry, the orange and red ash from the used cigarette to ignite the new one. Fifteen minutes and three cigarettes later we arrived at the shooting range. I had one foot on the running board before the GMC came to a complete stop.

"Slow down a second lightning, we've got plenty of time."

He put the truck in gear and pressed the emergency brake with his left foot. I grabbed the brown paper bag of shotgun shells and he took the gun case from behind the seat. We walked together through the screen door of the makeshift office to a weathered looking man. He had tan leathery skin, a receding hairline and a forehead that was riddled with wrinkles. His name was Henry. I had met him plenty of times before and was very familiar with his quirky and dry sense of humor.

"Bob, are you here to put on another show?"

Henry was the owner of the firing range. He like most people in our town seemed to know my dad on a first name basis. Henry knew better than most that dad was a champion sharpshooter. He was winner of the county fair clay-shooting contest for the last four years.

"No, it's my boy's turn today. He turns fourteen on Sunday."

"Fourteen, shit what I wouldn't give to be fourteen again. Fourteen is a big step you know? A boy can get his driver's license at fourteen", Henry said in a raspy tone.

Henry's animated reaction brought a large smile to dad's face.

"You don't need to tell him Henry, he's been reminding me since the day after he turned thirteen."

"Well driving is freedom and we all love the taste of freedom don't we?"

"It's gonna be a while before I can afford a car."

"Oh yeah. Maybe your old man here will get you one."

"Hang on Henry, he's got time."

"I suppose you're right. I thought I could give the boy some friendly advice."

Dad seemed amused by Henry's sudden interest in my fourteenth birthday. He leaned back and relaxed taking in the spectacle.

"Well first things first. Have you got a girlfriend yet?"

"No sir", I shyly responded.

"Well when you hit fourteen girls start looking a lot more like women than they do girls. You can't be taking them on any dates riding a ten speed bicycle. You know what I mean?"

"Sir?"

"If you want a girlfriend then you're gonna need a car. Don't matter what color the car is or how pretty the thing is, girls your age, they'll be impressed when you pull up in their driveway in your own set of wheels."

"We're not going car shopping tomorrow so don't feed the flames too much Henry."

Dad wasn't mad at Henry, in fact he was laughing at the advice Henry was dishing me since it was no secret that Henry was a lifelong bachelor and here he was handing out dating advice as if he were some sort of expert.

"Listen son, has your dad talked to you about the birds and the bees yet?"

"Jesus Henry", dad blurted out.

Dad was blushing and a little embarrassed by the last question.

"Now hang on Bob. This is important information that he's gonna need."

"Henry, what's that got to do with buying a car?"

"Listen and learn."

Henry turned his attention back to me. I found myself starting to giggle to the ridiculous nature of the conversation.

"Here's the thing. When you decide to get a car first off it don't have to be pretty. Second, the car don't have to be new. It just needs to have a decent stereo and four doors. Sedans have a bigger back seat. Ya know what I'm getting at?"

Dad had heard enough. Even though everything was good natured Henry was entering a topic area that was growing increasing uncomfortable for everybody except Henry.

"Thank you Henry. I'm sure the boy will take your advice to heart."

Dad smiled at Henry as he corralled me toward the firing range. My father then did what he always did at the firing range; he ended up putting on quite a show that afternoon. He was flawless. It did not matter which angle the clay pigeons came from or how quickly they followed each other. He shot them all. The hard clay discs exploded into tiny harmless fragments of clay and scattered across the pastureland.

Dad watched me while I shot and coached me when I had finished. I struggled mightily. Several sets of clay pigeons safely made passage over the fading horizon. My shotgun firing at every clay pigeon and most times the hard clay disc safely eluded the pellets.

That was why we were here though, so that I could learn, so that maybe someday I could be as good of a marksman as my father. That was going to be a challenge because few men could shoot a shotgun as well as my dad.

Dad never once became impatient while teaching me. He never once made me feel as if I was failing even though fake bird after fake bird made their way safely in front of me. At the end of the day, I had hit a total of three clay pigeons. Dad was thrilled, while I was humbled.

We tucked the gun case back behind the seat of the truck and made our way home. We had used all four boxes of ammunition. My ego was a little bruised but that wasn't what mattered. I was slowly easing closer to manhood. That's what mattered to me the most. It was not the number of clay pigeons that I had blasted from the sky. What was important was that I was sitting next to my superhero and I was one small step closer to being him.

Dad lit another cigarette and I looked out the passenger window and observed thousands of small green plants pushing their way through the dark black surface of the tilled fields. Everything that had happened so far that day made me believe that fourteen years old was going to be a very special time for me. I wanted to hold onto the moment for eternity, always keeping its picture fresh in my mind. The same way that dad holds the memories of his boyhood farmhouse in his mind. I pledged that I would never let that day escape my memory.

I turned my head back to the left. Dad glanced down at me and he was smiling joyfully. He gave me one of his patented quick winks and then rubbed his right hand over my head messing my hair. He inhaled deeply from his cigarette and I inhaled deeply taking in the fresh spring air as I stuck my head out the partially rolled down window. The wind blew across my face and I held my hand outside of the window frame feeling the cool air rush over my skin. I had goose bumps. Ahead of us in the distance I could see the sun beginning to set as it turned the horizon into a curtain of pink and orange. I closed my eyes again and inhaled the cool country air anxious for my birthday to arrive, so that I could officially be fourteen.

Chapter 6

We pulled up the rutty gravel driveway of our house. I saw our old green Plymouth sedan parked in front of the garage so I knew my mom was home. I could not wait to tell her about my day, that I had shot three of those elusive clay pigeons.

I ran inside anxious to share every detail of our afternoon. I rounded the corner of the living room and whisked into the kitchen. Mom was sitting at the kitchen table with the telephone pinned between her ear and her shoulder. She immediately held out her left hand extending her left index finger. It was her classic sign language symbol for "shush". A cup of black coffee breathed a steady stream of steam in front of her.

"Yes. Everything will be fine. Just relax. I know. I know. Well what do you want me to do? Be patient. I know. I have to go. I have to go! I'll talk to you later. Okay. Bye."

My mother never fully lost that big city girl that lived inside of her. She dressed in department store dresses high heeled shoes and bright red lipstick every day even though we lived on the outskirts of a small town where she might go the entire week without seeing a stranger at the house.

She primped every morning to keep her hair and makeup perfect. Her appearance was in direct contrast to the dusty earth toned landscape that we lived in. Appearance was everything to my mother and she was always dressed like a Manhattan housewife. She was a pretty woman that had aged extremely well but even so, she was still lacking in confidence.

The dresses that draped over her so elegantly and the lipstick that called attention to her face were nothing more than two pieces to her daily worn costume. It was a clever disguise and a way for her to hide her insecurities.

I was a teenager but I knew about self-confidence and the body language carried out beneath her flawless exterior told a very different story than the slender and attractive woman seated in front of me.

My mother's smiles were often forced and so was her laughter. I had been witness to her natural smiles and laughter and knew when they were genuine and when they were not. In reality her genuine laughter had been mostly absent for several years now. The pretend laughter was so easily detectable that I'm uncertain how she was not aware of its transparency.

Our conversations were usually short and one-sided. She rarely asked me about what I was learning in school or about the dozens of books she had seen me toting around the house. Our conversations weren't even conversations really, they were directives.

"Don't forget to cut the grass. Go take the laundry off the clothesline."

Her directives were impersonal quips that an employer might give to a cleaning staff or that a sergeant might bark at a private.

Our relationship had changed in other ways as well over the past couple of years. It had become more distant since she had rekindled her interest in the church. I was sure I knew her motives for having been so immersed in the activities at church. My theory was that she was desperately trying to fill a void that dwelled inside of her. Religion had been her most recent attempt at masking her inner feelings and defining her purpose. She needed a deeper fulfillment than being a wife and a mother. After all, when the streaks had been cleaned from the windows and the floor shimmered like a piece of glass, she was left with just herself, her thoughts and a spotlessly clean home.

For some people this might be satisfying but for my mother that made her extremely uncomfortable. For my mother keeping her thoughts company was akin to being naked in front of a full-length mirror. You're forced to see yourself with every physical flaw open to inspection. It was that eternal insecurity of my mother that lived just below the surface of her skin that patiently waited for her to be alone with her feelings so it could spring itself on her.

I waited just long enough to see the phone receiver return to its resting spot before exploding in a verbal volcano of words.

"Mom you're not going to believe this. We went out to the firing range and I was nervous but I did it. I shot three clay pigeons and I was real close to a bunch more. Oh, it is the best birthday present ever. Thank you!"

I almost ran out of breath before spitting out the final few words. I leaned forward to give her a hug. She had a blank and confused expression on her face and slipped her hands in between our bodies and pushed me back to an upright position without embracing me.

"What birthday present? Your birthday isn't until Sunday."

Her response was one of confusion and was laden with disgust. It left me thoroughly confused.

"The shotgun", I said in a matter of fact tone.

"Shotgun?"

A look of disappointment washed over her face.

The screen door snapped closed behind my dad as he came into the house. Mom pushed by me, out of the kitchen and into the living room to meet him at the front door.

"I just heard about Tommy's birthday present."

"He loves it. He's been walking on clouds all afternoon. You should have seen him out there."

"You know damn well how I feel about guns", my mother said rather angrily.

"Honey, I've been promising him since he was eight that when he turned fourteen he could have his own gun so he could go hunting with us. It's okay; I've already laid down the ground rules. He can't use the gun unless I'm with him."

The tone of mom's voice expressed the fury that her words did not express.

"Don't you think we should have discussed this?"

"There's nothing to discuss, I'm telling you everything is okay", my father responded in a somewhat frustrated voice.

My parents never had screaming matches but they had no shortage of disagreements. This one was minor. Mom was not that upset. If she had been, she would have asked me to go outside until they had finished talking. Instead, she went back into the kitchen, got her sweater off the back of a chair and headed toward the front door.

"Where are you going?"

"It's Thursday, I have bible study and then I have to help Pastor Jim prepare Sunday's lecture. There is a meatloaf in the oven and salad in the fridge. I won't be too late. I'll see you when I get back."

Ugh, Pastor Jim I thought to myself. He was the newest pastor at the church my mother attended. Pastors at that church came and went as often as the summers did it seemed. They usually left after only a year.

Pastor Jim was a Southerner and a former Baptist minister. I had met him a couple of times when I was with my mom running errands around town. I didn't care for him too much. He had made a poor first impression and the subsequent dozen times or so our paths crossed hadn't been much better.

Pastor Jim in my estimation was a phony. He was one of those persons who would ask you, "how are you" and by the time you finished answering the question they had already lost eye contact. He was one-half small town politician and one-half used car salesman. I say that partly because of how he dressed in three piece suits with shiny neckties in bold and obnoxious patterns and colors, and partly because he was missing that Midwestern genuine nice. His nice was unnatural. I could see through it but for some reason my mother couldn't. She was somehow fooled by the combination of Pastor Jim's flashy clothes and his manufactured personality.

His hair bothered me too. It was shiny and slicked back. Every strand of hair was in its perfect position and impervious to wind, rain and snow. The first few times I had met Pastor Jim I witnessed him pressing the sides of his hair with the palms of his hands, making sure that each strand was secure and in its proper place.

I watched Pastor Jim as he checked his reflection in a window of the church. He stopped, admiring his hair first and then used his hands as he worked down the front of his suit jacket to the waistband of his pants making sure that every piece of clothing was in its proper place. He pivoted from side to side checking his profile's reflection. He did a final inspection of his perfectly straight teeth by pushing his lips to his gum line and then when he was comfortable with how he looked he turned to face our direction.

Damn! I had spent a moment too long reflecting on Pastor Jim and my mother had slipped past me, out the front door and into the Plymouth.

"Mom, wait."

I hollered in vain from the front porch but it was too late. She couldn't hear me. The headlights of the Plymouth were already sweeping across the driveway by the time I opened the screen door as she was steering the car in a half circle away from our house.

I stood on the porch and watched as she sped away down the gravel road toward County Road 86.

Dad walked up behind me and put his hands on my shoulders.

"Come on, let's eat."

It was an imperfect ending to what had otherwise been a perfect summer day. Guilt consumed me. I wondered if my mother felt like an outsider. I had recently become so much closer to my dad than I was to her. I wondered if that bothered her. I went into the kitchen and joined him at the kitchen table. It had been such a great day. I was three days away from becoming fourteen, three days closer to that imaginary line that I called manhood.

Chapter 7

The morning of my fourteenth birthday my father took me out and taught me how to drive his truck. Since it was a stick shift it made it even that much more of a challenge for me. He was patient and I was erratic. The truck lurched to a stop repeatedly as I released the clutch too quickly causing the truck to lurch forward and killing the engine. Nevertheless, he sat in the passenger seat relaxed and smiling. One time my foot slipped off of the clutch pedal causing the engine to kill and moved him forward so violently that he bumped his head on the windshield. The collision knocked the lit cigarette out of his mouth and onto the truck seat between his legs. He rubbed the top of his head with his right hand and snuffed out the cigarette with his left hand.

I felt horrible and I began to apologize profusely. As suddenly as I had popped the clutch he exploded into a loud and boisterous laughter that brought me to ease. Dad's deep laughter was contagious and in no time I joined him laughing hysterically, stalled on the road. I don't know if it is possible but I think he was having more fun than I was. He stopped laughing just long enough to ask me a question.

"Not as easy as it looks is it?"

We stayed on the back roads where the only people who were in danger were my father and I. It wasn't too long after that incident that I started to get the hang of driving his truck. The starts became smoother and we drove the rural roads for a couple of hours until I felt comfortable shifting gears and learned how to move the truck forward from a dead stop.

That afternoon after we arrived back at our house, we celebrated my birthday with my uncles Art and Earl, my uncle Tommy's widow aunt Gloria and my cousins Joey and Junior.

I proudly showed my cousins my shotgun and after dinner all of us played a game of wiffleball on the lawn behind the house. When we weren't playing the adults sat at the picnic table reminiscing of times gone by and occasionally bursting into spontaneous laughter.

Meanwhile while the rest of us were outside enjoying ourselves my mother kept herself secluded inside of the house doing busy work. Aunt Gloria went inside and helped her with the dishes and cleaning up. Mom was quiet despite my Aunt's attempts to engage her in conversation.

Aunt Gloria stepped back outside to join the rest of us. She pulled a cold bottle of beer from under the melting cubes of ice in the cooler. It was the something that you would never witness my mother doing, drinking a cold beer from a brown bottle. Aunt Gloria had something that my mother didn't have however that allowed her to do something so blue collar as to drink no name beer straight from a bottle. The difference between my mother and my Aunt Gloria was that Aunt Gloria had self-esteem. Gloria was happy to be surrounded by a loving extended family that had held her closely.

Aunt Gloria was carefree and loved playing with my cousins and me. She volunteered to be the pitcher in our game of wiffleball. She wasn't afraid to get her hands dirty or play rough. In fact, she was comfortable being barefoot and running through the yard like a carefree teenager. It was the type of thing I had never seen my mother do. It just wasn't "ladylike" to be in a pair of cutoff blue jean shorts and a faded tee shirt playing ball with the boys.

From the corner of my eye I could see my mother watching us from between the curtains of the kitchen window as we played. Maybe she was a little envious of my Aunt Gloria. Maybe she wished that she could let her guard down long enough to not worry whether someone were to see her without any makeup and with a little dirt under her fingernails.

I waved to her and she waved back but she looked unhappy and tearful. She quickly turned away and I watched as the back of her head moved away from the window and out of view.

The game continued on with my mother making an occasional appearance outside. She played the role of good hostess but she never sat down or stopped long enough to have a conversation of any substance. Her unwillingness to socialize and her conspicuous absence bothered me but it wasn't about to spoil an event that I had anticipated for 364 days.

As nightfall approached, family members left the house one carload at a time. For me it would be a mostly sleepless night. I reached over to my nightstand and turned on my AM radio. I did what I did on many nights when I was unable to sleep; I tuned in and listened to Larry King. Maybe Larry's show could help me fall asleep. I enjoyed lying in my bed and listening to Larry King especially when he talked baseball.

I lay there with my eyes open and my stomach stuffed to the point of near misery. I had to keep reminding myself that I was fourteen years old. Fourteen changed everything.

I sat up in bed and looked out the window at the full moon and the many stars that surrounded it. The plastic wiffeball bat rested peacefully in the tall grass next to the picnic table. A rabbit darted around the yard freezing like a statue occasionally.

I sat back down on my bed and switched my focus to the wall at the end of my bed. My birthday present was hanging there so proudly. Mounted on the wall was a gun rack that had been made by my father in his workshop. It hung on the wall and my Browning twenty gauge was nestled firmly in the felt lined holders. Why would anyone want to keep such a beautiful gun in a dirty old broken down gun case? My shotgun was like a piece of art to me. It was beautiful with its dark cherry stock and charcoal barrel. The gun rack was almost the same color as the stock of the gun. Dad had kept it hidden in the garage rafters wrapped in an old quilt.

I swung my legs over the side of the bed and quietly stood up in the mostly darkened room. I walked over to the gun rack, reached up, and picked the shotgun out of its resting place. I returned with the gun in my hands to the side of my bed and admired the cold smooth metal barrel as I ran my fingers along it. I pumped the gun, raised it to my shoulder, and began picking various inanimate objects from around the room and pretended to shoot them as I brought them in line for a shot.

I aimed at a lamp that sat on my dresser, gently squeezed the trigger and quietly whispered "bang" to myself. I moved the gun upward and located a plane that was gently suspended from the corner of the ceiling. Once it was squarely in my view I again squeezed on the trigger blowing up one more toy in my make believe shooting gallery.

I lowered the gun again to my waist. This time I pumped the shotgun and quickly raised the barrel while sizing up a poster of a Rod Carew, a baseball player that hung on the inside of my bedroom door. Just as I was about to squeeze the trigger my bedroom door swung open and my father quickly took cover as he saw the muzzle of the gun staring him down.

"Jesus Tommy. What are you doing?"

My dad just about jumped out of his boxer shorts upon seeing the end of the shotgun pointed in his direction.

"I'm just practicing."

"Yeah well you just scared the crap out of me."

Dad chuckled which helped to lighten the mood and ease the tension that had briefly built.

"I know you're excited, but I have to be up early tomorrow and I can hear you moving around in here. Put that thing away and get some sleep would you? It's late."

I quickly sprang to my feet and returned the gun to the gun rack on the wall.

Dad shook his head and smiled. "Good night."

"Good night dad. Thank you. It was the best birthday ever."

Dad winked at me and closed the bedroom door.

I turned the radio volume slightly lower and picked an unspent shotgun shell off of my nightstand. I twirled it between my fingers as I stared upward at the ceiling.

My first night as a fourteen year old was nearing its end. My eyes were finally growing heavy. I watched the shadow that was cast from the spinning shotgun shell as it moved between my fingers. The shadow was slowly hypnotizing me into a deep sleep. I was fourteen. I was unconquerable.

Chapter 8

I'm not sure what time I finally fell asleep that night but it was very early the next morning when I was awoken. The sky was still black and the sun had not yet rose above the horizon line. The full moon I had watched as my eyes fell weary the night before had changed positions and now sat low in the Western sky. I was in a deep sleep, a small pool of drool soaked into my pillowcase as I lay on my side facing the wall away from my bedroom door.

A large strong hand firmly gripped onto my right shoulder.

"Tommy, wake up."

I must be dreaming I thought to myself, I tugged on the thin cotton blanket that covered my legs pulling it closer toward my chin.

"Tommy come on, it's time to get up."

Startled I immediately rolled to a position where I was lying flat on my back. I rubbed my eyes trying to adjust to the blackness of the room. My dad had awoken me. He was sitting on the side of my bed.

"What's wrong?"

"Nothing is wrong. How would you like to come to work with me today?"

My mind was still in a fog and I hadn't fully comprehended what my father had just asked.

"It's still dark out", I said groggily.

"You want to buy a car right? You're going to need some money to do that so now that you are fourteen you can come and work with me, at least for this summer."

I rubbed my eyes again. I was in a state of half sleep and half wake.

"Come on get up. I'll tell you about it over breakfast but you have to eat quickly. We need to be on the road by six."

Dad got up and left the bedroom.

I blindly walked to my dresser and grabbed a pair of blue jeans, a tee shirt and a pair of tube socks. I wandered into the bathroom brushed my teeth and ran my hands under the sink faucet and then used them to wet my hair straight. A few minutes later, I was eating scrambled eggs with my father and listening to him as he told me about how he hoped I would come to work with him for the summer and learn carpentry.

Without any hesitation, I said "yes".

Dad flashed a big smile, big enough that I noticed some tiny wrinkles that radiated from the corners of his eyes for the first time. It was a change in his appearance that I had never noticed before."

"Let's hit the road kiddo. I got more roofing jobs than I know what to do with right now. We got to stop by and pick up a couple more hands to help us."

Dad often needed day laborers. He used men from the local halfway house. He made arrangements the day before and then would simply stop by with his pickup in the morning and pick up as many men as he would need for that day to work. He paid the men each week and could hire the men on an "as needed" basis without having to bring on full-time employees.

The two men who had been helping my dad most recently were both Native American Sioux Indians.

Dad put the key in the ignition and turned over the engine. With the truck idling smoothly he reached into his shirt pocket and fished out a cigarette. He stuck it in his mouth and began speaking to me as dug into his pants pocket for his lighter.

"These guys we're picking up look a little rough around the edges but don't let them scare you. They'd rather be out with us working than trapped inside the dingy walls of the halfway house."

Dad finally pulled his lighter from his pants pocket and with a flick of his thumb brought a flame to the cigarette and puffed it to life. With smoke swirling inside of him he continued to speak while small clouds of smoke expelled and punctuated with each word.

"The older guys name is Rich. He doesn't say too much but he's a good carpenter and I never have to tell him what to do, he's always looking for more work to do."

Dad brought the cigarette from his mouth to the ashtray and tapped it shaking the ashes loose from the end of it.

"The other guy, well actually he's really just a kid, his name is Carl but I call him Easy. He's really shy. Don't be surprised if he doesn't speak to you at all. It's nothing personal he just keeps to himself mostly."

Dad brought the truck to a stop along the curb in front of a large brick building with tall white columns and a matching brick stoop. The halfway house appeared to be a converted apartment building.

The two men my father had just described to me were sitting with their legs dangling over the edge of the stoop waiting to be picked up. They stood up slowly and began walking toward the truck. Both of them had slender builds and wore long dark black braided ponytails. Carl or "Easy" as my father had begun calling him was smiling and the shorter of the two. As he got closer I could see that his face was badly pockmarked with acne scars. He was wearing a white tee shirt and a pair of raggedy Wrangler blue jeans. Rich was older looking than Carl and not as thin. He was riddled with greenish blue tattoos that ran up and down his arms from his wrists to his shoulders. The tattoos were a mixture of words spelled in calligraphic letters and block print along with an array of pictures that didn't seem to belong together.

I didn't realize that I had been staring until my eyes locked the gaze of Easy's eyes. I froze as he caught me off guard. Rich and Easy climbed over the fender wells and into the box of the pickup. They sat down with their backs against the cab facing the tailgate. Easy gave a quick double tap on the roof of the cab signaling to my dad that they were ready to go.

As my father steered the truck back out onto the street he looked over at me possibly to gauge my reaction to the men he had just picked up.

"Dad, what did they do to get in trouble?"

I was curious. The way they carried themselves was so timid and they were deafeningly quiet.

"I don't know for sure", Dad quickly replied. "Let's just say they made some really bad decisions."

Dad paused to take a drag off his cigarette. He then tapped on the window glass that separated us from them. Easy turned his head to see what my father wanted. He held his pack of cigarettes and a lighter up, a symbolic gesture to see if either of them wanted a cigarette as well. Easy nodded "yes" and my father held the cigarettes and the lighter in his left hand outside the window and around the side of the pickup cab. Easy stood up and took the pack of cigarettes and lighter from my father's hand as we cruised down the road.

Dad brought his arm back inside of the truck. The men cupped their hands helping each other so they could get the lighter flame to the cigarette before the rush of air from the moving truck blew it out.

I turned my head back around looking at the road in front of us.

"All you got to do son is treat them like you would anyone else. You'll be surprised how far that'll get you."

My father had a genuine compassion for these men. He knew that few people would give them a second chance and even fewer would be able to put them to work knowing their history. Dad understood that they were free spirits and many times rebelled against the white people like us that had spent a century trying to force our culture on them.

Dad was in the midst of several roofing jobs. A late spring hailstorm had produced a backlog of work. If dad had been farming the storm might have meant devastation to a crop that was just starting to stand above the dry black topsoil but since he had chosen carpentry as his career the storm was instead a financial windfall.

Dad pulled onto a long cement drive and drove past the rear side of the house. Rich and Easy stood up in the box of the pickup and began unloading the tools that my father had packed in that part of the truck. They stacked the tools neatly in a spot behind the house. Rich leaned an extension ladder against the eave of the roof and Easy began putting together a set of three tool belts. I watched Easy as he put a crowbar, hammer and a generous supply of roofing nails in the pocket of each tool belt.

When I looked up again my dad was opening the driver side door of his truck and sitting down in front of the steering wheel.

"Dad."

I quickly made my way over to the rolled down passenger door window frame.

"Where are you going?"

"I have to go into town. I have some business to take care of. Just do what they tell you to do and I'll be back as quick as I can."

Dad started the pickup and shouted out to Rich and Easy from the cab of the pickup.

"Show him the ropes guys. He's a smart kid and a quick learner but he doesn't know diddly shit about pounding a nail or putting on a shingle so expect a lot of questions and show him the right way to get the job done. Understood?"

"You got it Bob", Rich hollered back.

I walked back over to the base of the ladder that was leaned against the roof.

"Here you go kid."

Easy had assembled a tool belt for me and was holding it out like a welcome gift.

"Wear that around your waste like this."

Easy showed me how he had fastened the tool belt to keep it snugly in place while he moved about.

"You first", Rich said in a firm tone.

Rich's head gazed upward toward the roof.

I hesitantly stepped forward, took one deep breath and proceeded to climb the ladder rung by rung being careful not to look downward. At the top I sat down on the side of the roof leaving room for Easy and Rich to get past me as they joined me on the brittle and worn weather beaten shingles.

I leaned forward and looked down toward the grass.

"What's the matter? Are you afraid of heights", Rich asked.

"I've been to the top of the water tower", I responded trying to hide my fear of heights.

"Really, did you put any shingles on it?"

I didn't know if Rich was trying to be funny with his sarcastic remark or if he was busting my balls because he saw me as a hindrance more than a help.

Easy quickly changed the subject.

"Let me give you a couple of pointers", Easy said.

Easy pointed in the direction of two power lines that were dangling dangerously close to my head.

"Touch one of those and you can kiss your ass goodbye."

I immediately began moving away from the droopy power line. As I did so I lost my footing and began a slide down the worn shingles. There was nothing to grab onto as I gained speed sliding face up. Just before I reached the edge of the roof Easy reached out and grabbed my arm. My legs swung over the side of the roof and Easy's grip on my sweaty forearm was anything but secure. He quickly reached with his free hand and with two hands now wrapped around my arm and wrist he dug his heels into the moist shingles and let out a loud groan as he pulled me back to the base of the roof. Easy was deceptively strong for his slight build. He let out a rather loud exhale. I sat a couple feet away from him still dazed by the sudden turn of events. I carefully leaned over to see where I could have fallen had Easy not had such quick reflexes.

"That's another thing", Easy said rather calmly considering what had just happened.

"These shingles get wet from the morning dew so watch your footing. It's humid and most of the grit is worn off of them."

I expelled a large breath of air.

"Thank you. You saved my ass," I said smiling.

"Just be careful. I don't need you to get hurt the same day that your dad trusted us to look after you."

I spent the rest of the morning learning how to prepare a roof that had several layers of old worn out shingles nailed to it. Easy and Rich helped show me how to use my crowbar to tear loose the old shingles. It was the first step in preparing the roof. I was timidly prying the shingles loose at first but after more coaching by Easy it wasn't long before I was ripping away the shingles and tossing them to the ground below me. Rich, Easy and I took up position on the roof and systematically stripped it down to the tar paper. Once we finished the first side of the roof we moved to the other side.

I repeated that first day of work morning after morning from one job site to another. I did almost everything from that first day of work including nailing the shingle nails to the roofs. I was also busy doing cleanup, setting up scaffolding, moving bundles of shingles and getting Rich and Easy whatever they needed to get the job done.

The humidity was smothering at times and the sun unrelenting when it wasn't hiding behind a blanket of clouds. As the days passed by I was growing both physically and mentally stronger.

I had a new found appreciation for what my father had been doing all these years. I remember the nights that my father would come home after a twelve-hour day and still have the energy to toss a baseball to me. On other evenings after a long day of work we would head up to the river and do some fishing. The nights that he didn't spend with me, he was busy doing bookkeeping, bids, and scheduling for his business. Despite his demanding schedule I never once heard him complain. This was the life he had chosen. He was in control of his own destiny just as he had wanted and he wasn't about to complain about the responsibility that came along with the pursuit of his dream.

Chapter 9

Summer break was breezing along. The first six weeks had passed quickly and waking up at five thirty in the morning had become much easier. Everyday I was learning and every day I was bonding a little more with Easy. Rich had found his way back into prison through a path that started at the inside of a whiskey bottle. He went on a drinking binge according to Easy and didn't check back in to the halfway house for four days. The police found him twenty miles away after he shoplifted some beer at a gas station.

Easy was sympathetic to Rich but unemotional at the same time. That wasn't unusual as he had said very little to me over the first several weeks I had known him. Slowly he and I learned a little bit more about each other and Easy began to open up and allowed me to get to know him on a personal level.

Easy grew up on an Indian reservation in Flandreau, South Dakota. I also learned that Easy was an alcoholic since he had been a teenager. Before he went to prison his sobriety was fleeting. When he was a teenager getting alcohol was a simple task, Easy told me that he would steal whiskey from his foster dad's liquor stash. He was smart enough to never take the whole bottle. Instead he would siphon off a few ounces at a time which went unnoticed by his foster dad who was busy battling his own demons. His foster dad would not only forget how much liquor was left in his already opened liquor bottle but almost everything else that had happened the prior evening.

Alcoholism was a new and difficult concept for me to understand. My dad had let me take a sip from one of his beers once and the taste was so bitter and uninviting that I had no interest in tasting it again. I couldn't imagine why anyone would ever choose a beer over a soda. It was no contest to me, soda had a better taste.

I was fourteen and even though I was feeling more like a man and less like a child I was still naïve. I didn't understand that drinking for an alcoholic was not about taste or pleasure. It was about suppression, depression, and an escape from the realities of a person's past and present.

For someone like me who had led what most people would agree had been a very normal life up to this point I only needed a good book to escape.

While I escaped through reading, Easy escaped from the dysfunctional childhood that he was immersed in one sip at a time until his mind was numb and the mental pain that he had experienced became blurred and then eventually temporarily forgotten.

My father served not only as Easy's employer but also as his counselor and his surrogate father. Easy trusted my father and began confiding in him, which helped him to maintain his sobriety. When he was feeling the compulsion to drink, he talked to my father about his urges, which was a new alternative escape to the whiskey and cheap beer, which he had previously relied upon.

In conversation as we were working Easy told me that my father had cured him of the shame he had carried with him since he was a young boy. Easy was convinced that if it were not for my dad drinking would be his occupation, not working as a carpenter. He said he would likely have ended up returning to the only way he knew to cope with the daily stresses of life.

As a result of my father's faith in him, Easy developed a loyalty that was unquestionable. Easy's loyalty in turn furthered my father's respect toward him. Easy became more willing to speak openly about his parentless childhood and the resulting instability that dwelled at the core of his inner self. It was an instability born out of the experience of having been raised by a series of foster families.

Easy told me that his life was more stable right now than it had been at any other previous time. Because of my father's handling of Easy, he in turn treated me more like a younger brother and less like the teenage son of the man he was working for. He teased me and challenged me by seeing if I could keep up with his rapid pace of work.

Easy's upbringing had prematurely aged him making him look older than he really was. His skin was weathered and pock marked. He wasn't very tall and he was extremely skinny. He told me that he was twenty years old, only six years older than I was.

He liked to test my strength and toughness with the work we were doing and also through a game he called bloody knuckles that we played sometimes on break.

He rotated two pairs of jeans and three tank tops. It was his entire summer wardrobe. Some days he would wear a red bandana to catch the sweat and keep it from running down his brow and burning his eyes.

There was one and only one constant with Easy, a silver and turquoise necklace in the shape of a cross that he wore every day. For a person with nothing of material value he treasured that necklace. It had little monetary value but nothing of Easy's did. This necklace held value for one reason only. It had once belonged to his father. Not his foster father but rather his own biological father. It was the only physical connection that Easy had to the past that he couldn't remember and a father he would never know.

Easy and I quickly became friends during those first six weeks of summer. I had few friends at school. It was a small school to begin with and living in the country like we did there were few classmates in close proximity to our house.

Easy had few friends because of his internal instincts, which acted as a protective shield from the evil and the pain that the outside world had subjected him to throughout his childhood. Giving trust to a stranger or even someone like me that he had known for a short time equated to vulnerability to him. Unfortunately that was what he had learned during the twenty short years that he had been alive.

His lack of trust eventually gave way during a lunch break on one of those humid summer days. Easy opened up and explained why he had ended up in the Halfway House.

We sat as we usually did during lunch with Easy, my father and I side by side on the tailgate of the pickup. My father had never asked Easy about his past and he never expected him to volunteer why he ended up in the halfway house. If Easy ever decided to speak of the skeletons that he had hidden in his closet it would have to be initiated by him.

It turns out Easy had spent most of his teenage life incarcerated. Lunchtime conversation was usually light and reserved for current events, the weather or occasionally a tale as only my father could tell. However, on this afternoon Easy was about to enter uncharted territory and speak to us about what had led him to be incarcerated.

"I'm happy you took a chance on me Bob. I really enjoy doing this kind of work."

The comment appeared to catch my father off guard but his reply was truthful and quick.

"Easy you may find this hard to believe but from day one I never felt like I was taking a chance on you. I needed help and you proved to be a hard worker. It seems to me like I got the better end of the deal."

"Well, it means a lot to me. A lot of people are afraid of someone like me, an ex-con. They think everyone in prison is rotten on the inside but we're not all evil. I'm not saying I didn't deserve to be punished for what I did but I wouldn't have done anything differently if I had to make the same choices today as I did back then."

Easy went on to explain how it all started years earlier when he was about my age. He had spent years bouncing from foster family to foster family until he ended up as one of six foster children in a less than perfect foster home. Easy had a small frame and had a slight build, which was not much of a challenge for his foster dad who was a physically imposing figure.

His foster dad was a barrel-chested mechanic who worked on cars in a large steel garage outside of the house they lived in, that is when he wasn't sleeping off the effects of his last quart of cheap southern whiskey he had downed.

The foster children were important to his foster parents for one reason and one reason only. The foster children were a steady source of income, a way for the family to pay their bills. His foster dad reminded Easy and the rest of the foster children often that they were living with them because they had been unwanted and abandoned by their real parents. He used fear and intimidation and when that didn't work he used the hot tip of his cigarette to remind each of the children who was in control.

As Easy spoke in a monotone voice, I noticed my father develop an unmistakable look of concern like I had never seen before. His expression remained unchanged during the narrative except for a slight grimace when Easy turned his back to us and lifted his sweat soaked tank top.

Easy's back was a road map of his lost childhood illustrated by the multitude of scars and puckered areas of raised skin. He had suffered through years of abuse believing that he was living with the only family that would have him. With his self esteem nowhere to be found Easy held on to that belief until one night when he was fourteen years old.

It was on that fateful night that Easy was sitting in his bedroom reading a book when he overheard his foster dad speaking to his foster mom about one of his younger brothers. It didn't matter that it wasn't a blood relative they were speaking of, to Easy the foster brother was his sibling and he felt a responsibility to be his protector.

His foster brother had been in trouble at school again. His foster mother tried to reason with his foster dad but when his foster father was drunk like he was on this night, there was no reasoning with him. He needed little excuse to exercise his internal demons by inflicting pain on the younger and more defenseless children. Easy knew what he had been subjected to in the last three years and he wanted no other children to live through the physical and emotional pain that he had experienced.

It was a sobering lesson for a child who as a teenager began to numb his feelings a few stolen ounces of whiskey at a time.

Easy felt trapped even though he knew his foster parents held no love for either him or his siblings. They were simply running a business, warehousing foster children and receiving a check each month for each child that they held hostage. He knew that he had to stop his foster dad but he wasn't sure how he could do that.

Easy was unable to sleep that night. He lay awake in the room he shared with two of his brothers. His mind was a virtual cinema as he replayed the past eight years of his life on a movie projector that churned inside of his head. He relived each cigarette burn, each bruise and each cruel word. As the night wore on, his hatred for the foster father who had tormented him grew stronger and stronger until the slamming of the front door startled him back to reality.

Easy raised his arm and held it in front of the moonlight that shimmered through the bedroom window. It was two in the morning according to the face of his wristwatch. His foster dad had just returned home from the bar and was clumsily making his way through the house in a drunken stupor. This was Act One of the abusive play that Easy had seen acted out upon himself so many times before. His eight-year-old foster brother was in for a man sized beating. It would be a one-sided onslaught that wouldn't be deterred by any amount of crying or pleading. Either his foster dad would physically tire and lose interest or the object of his anger would have to withstand the worst that his intolerable temper and his two-inch wide leather belt could deliver.

My father and I were fixated on Easy as he spoke. He stopped only briefly to wet his mouth with a quick drink from his stainless steel canteen and then he continued to tell his story.

Easy told us how he walked to the bedroom closet in the darkened room he shared with two foster siblings. He was quiet and careful not to make any noise. He slid the closet door along its tracks just wide enough to reach his arm inside and remove an aluminum baseball bat.

Easy was in a trance as he spoke to us. His mind was swimming with the memories of the piercing pain that had left each scar on his back. He still held the memory of the putrid stench of his own skin as the red-hot ashes of his foster dad's cigarette burned into it. He could remember biting into his bottom lip so hard that his teeth broke through the skin. He could still taste his own blood, as he lay crumpled on the carpet after he had received the powerful punch of his foster dad's clenched fist. He fought fiercely to hold in the tears that determinedly tried to force their way out of his eyes. It had been three years of pain and torment that had led Easy to remove the baseball bat from that closet that night. Those three years of anger and pain were about to climax with one furiously violent moment of rage.

Easy was no longer a helpless eleven year old that could be lied to, manipulated and intimidated. He was now a young man and he was about to extract his revenge while saving his foster siblings from enduring the pain and the beatings that he had suffered so many nights before.

Had his foster dad been sober that night, he might have been too great of a force for Easy to overcome but intoxicated as he was on this night, his foster dad was both uncoordinated and vulnerable.

Easy carefully opened the bedroom door and looked behind himself to make sure that his siblings were still sleeping. He turned sideways and squeezed himself between the doorframe and the wall until he was squarely in the hallway. A faint light filtered under the bottom of the kitchen door.

Easy took small and careful steps, the baseball bat gripped firmly in his left hand while his right hand worked like the whiskers on a cat guiding him along the cold plastered wall of the hallway. He walked on the balls of his feet trying to move as quietly as possible as his left foot crept in front of his right foot, step-by-step and inch-by-inch. His heart was pounding faster with each forward movement. His body was tense and his left hand was trembling from a combination of fear and anxiety that flooded inside of him. Suddenly he was energized by a rage driven rush of adrenalin.

Easy squeezed the handle of the bat with all of the strength and determination he could muster. He had finally reached the white raised panel door that led into the kitchen.

Inside of the kitchen his foster dad sat on a folding chair at the kitchen table. He was alone except for a half empty bottle of Black Velvet, which sat on the kitchen table in front of him waiting to be consumed.

Easy had made up his mind, he wasn't turning back. He had hoped that his foster dad would be seated alone in the kitchen. He listened quietly at the door waiting to hear a second voice. There was no other voice to be heard. That meant that his foster mom was most likely in the bedroom sleeping already or at least pretending to be sleeping to stay clear of the highly combustible lump of flesh and bone that sat only a short distance away from where Easy stood frozen.

It would be a one on one confrontation, exactly as Easy had wanted it to be. His foster dad meandered about the kitchen talking to himself and mumbling incoherently as he took an ice tray out of the freezer. He managed to get part of the cubes into a glass while a few other cubes hit the kitchen floor and slid away harmlessly across the dirty linoleum.

Easy took one final deep breath, squeezed his eyes closed momentarily for a brief prayer and then placed his right hand on the door handle. He quietly turned the door knob and calmly walked through the entrance and into the kitchen. He now stood just a few feet away from where his tormentor sat.

His foster dad either didn't see the baseball bat or at a minimum didn't understand its significance. He snarled in his usual ornery voice

"What are you doing up?"

Easy said nothing and flexed the fingers of his left hand on the bat handle making sure he had a solid grip.

"Are you deaf? Get back to bed before I kick your queer little Indian ass in there."

Easy knew that he was crossing a threshold, one from which there would be no return.

His foster dad was agitated by Easy's lack of response and puzzled by his lack of expression. Easy thought about speaking but what could he say that would change anything. He was standing in the face of evil, in front of a man who had already bullied and beat him on several occasions. A guiltless man who wasn't about to change the way he treated the foster children. If his foster dad had not felt compassion while he was administering one of his dozens of beatings he had handed out over the years then what could Easy say now that would possibly make him understand the scope of the damage that had resulted from his abuse. If you can torture a child without any remorse then maybe, just maybe you are one of those rare individuals who are born without a conscience and are not capable of feeling empathy, a sociopathic type.

"I ain't sayin' it again Carl. Get to bed now before I drag your sissy little ass in there by your ponytail."

To his foster family he was Carl. The nickname of "Easy" wouldn't be born until several years later when he came to work for my father.

His foster dad's eyes were fixated on Carl as he lifted a half empty glass of whiskey to his already intoxicated being. Without any warning, Easy slowly raised the handle of the baseball bat and struck a swift and powerful blow to the face of his nemesis. The bat smashed across his foster dad's fingertips first shattering the glass of whiskey and then landing soundly across his left ear.

The force of the swing knocked his foster dad and the chair he was sitting on sideways tipping them both over onto the cold vinyl floor. Easy stepped sideways and stared down at his foster dad, who was now lying on the floor and bleeding profusely.

Easy felt no sense of victory or remorse. His foster dad reached his hand back and felt behind his ear. He brought his hand back in front of his face rubbing the bright red blood between his fingertips. His advanced state of intoxication numbed what would otherwise be an unbearable amount of pain for any sober person.

He chuckled nervously through a set of stained and gritted teeth as he stared at Easy. Easy was unmoved by his foster dad's reaction and stared back calmly.

"Carl, you really messed up this time!"

His foster dad steadied himself to a position on his knees his left hand on the kitchen table and his bloody right hand clenched into a fist. He leaned slightly against the table trying to raise himself to his feet. Easy was no longer intimidated by the presence of his once mighty tormentor and swung again, quickly and forcefully. The blow was so violent that his foster dad crumpled like a flimsy aluminum beer can. A stream of blood flung from the corner of his mouth across the dirty white kitchen wall. He lost his balance and fell headfirst smashing his face against the table on the way down. He lay unconscious on the floor; blood running from his nose, mouth and ear.

With one final act of anger Easy kicked his foster dad in the midsection knocking the wind out of him and creating a thin mist of blood, which sprayed from his mouth. Easy then reached for the half smoked cigarette, which had dropped to the floor in the midst of the scuffle. He puffed on it bringing the cherry to a bright orange color. He pulled his foster dad's shirt loose from his jeans exposing his skin and then pressed the cigarette firmly into his back burning a hole into the fatty flesh. It was the perfect reminder for all the times that Easy had been scarred before in the same manner.

Easy was emotionally drained and physically exhausted as he finished telling us every detail of that life-changing event.

It was an unbelievable story yet I could tell that every word of it was true. Easy wasn't gleaming with pride and bravado. In fact, he was barely showing any emotion at all. He somberly hung his head and kicked at the dirt with his shoe, almost as if he was ashamed of his actions.

Each of us sat quietly in an awkward silence that lasted several moments until my father finally spoke relieving the tension and saying the words that Easy had been waiting to hear for most of his life.

"Life doesn't come with an instruction book, Easy. That's what makes living so hard sometimes, because you have to make difficult decisions and be willing to live with them. You've had a lot to overcome but you still get up every morning and you do what you have to. You're strong. You're spirit is strong. Now you have to let go of the past and push forward. Today is a new day."

My father had grabbed hold of Easy's attention. The words passed through Easy's ears and channeled directly into his core.

"Forgive yourself Easy. It's time to let go of the past. No more guilt, you've punished yourself enough already. You did what you had to do and let's be honest with each other, that son of a bitch got exactly what he deserved."

Easy finally crinkled a small smile of relief. It appeared that he was touched by what my father had said. Even so, he held onto his emotions, just as he had been taught to do his entire life.

However, that moment was a turning point for Easy. He was allowed to forgive himself for the first time since he had sought his revenge. He was finally part of a family and felt a sense of belonging. No longer would he be the scared and timid outsider that had masked his own feelings of guilt and shame with alcohol.

I will always remember that day when the bond was set between Easy and my father. We went back to work. Easy turned on the AM radio we brought to each job site. It was the same old country music that we listened to every day; Willie Nelson, Merle Haggard, Johnny Cash and a parade of blue collar crooners singing about the average guy and his struggles. Each song echoed through that dirty old AM radio that was crackling with static.

We each went back to work, without speaking for quite a while. I watched my dad dig his spade into the soft black dirt. He was winded, tired and sweating. A cigarette pinched between his lips, one third of it was ashes. He talked with the cigarette vibrating between his lips until the burnt ashes fell off the end and were blown away in the wind.

My dad finally broke the silence that had surrounded us since Easy had cleansed his soul.

"So what ever happened to that son of a bitch, Easy?"

Easy was working slowly, probably contemplating the guilt that had gripped him for so many years. He stopped digging and leaned on the end of his spade, exhaling deeply and staring at the ground silently. It was a long silence and then Easy finally lifted his head and looked at my dad.

"I really don't know. I didn't kill him so hopefully he realized how close he came to the end of the line. I'm sure he's still mean. I don't think a person like him can change. If he is dishing out his whippings on anyone smaller than him I hope every time he looks in a mirror and sees his crooked nose and his missing teeth. Maybe that way he'll think twice about loosening that belt from his pants."

Easy went back to digging the footings for the driveway we were building. Dad lit a new cigarette and I did what I could to help.

Easy finally freed himself from the internal demons that had tortured him for such a long time. It was a turning point for him. He would be less inclined to reach for a bottle when he was caught in a time warp of the dysfunctional childhood that he had endured. He no longer had to numb the guilt that would wash over him when his mind had time too much free time to think.

That single conversation would heal him more than a hundred years worth of drinks or a year in jail ever could. His spirit had been restored. His innocence, though still missing was at least within reach and most importantly the walls that he had built to protect himself were slowly crumbling and being dismantled, one cruel brick at a time.

It made me think a lot about my family and what I had, a mother and a father who cared about me. How I never went to sleep wondering who my parents were or why they had abandoned me. It was the kind of learning experience that a child can't learn in a classroom. It was a lesson about pain, sadness and the power of the human spirit. It was a story that I decided to share with my mother over dinner that evening.

Chapter 10

It had been a long and tiring day. I had learned the ritual that my father went through every evening after work. My mother had made it very clear. The work boots stayed on the front porch. The dirty clothes went straight to the washroom. It was a quick shower and then dinner. Mom was an impeccable housekeeper. The last thing she wanted was a set of muddy footprints across her floor.

We sat at the kitchen table, a less common occurrence recently. Tonight there were no prayer meetings, no bible studies and my mother would be joining my father and me for dinner. I was excited to tell her about my day at work and what I had done. I also wanted to tell her about Easy, about everything he had overcome in his life and the amazing story he had shared with dad and I.

Dinner was baked chicken, Swiss chard, mashed potatoes and sliced tomatoes. Mom took great pride in her cooking and with good reason. We sat quietly eating until mom broke the silence.

"What did you do to your hand?"

I had accidentally hit it with the hammer earlier that day.

"It's nothing."

Mom grabbed it and pulled it closer to her face for observation.

"It's purple."

I pulled it back not wanting to be babied over such a minor injury.

"It's fine. It doesn't even hurt."

My discolored thumbnail was a badge of honor for me. It had hurt when I had hit it but now it was just unsightly, the pain had long since dissipated. It was the type of injury I had seen on my father's hand dozens of times.

"Can Easy come and have dinner with us tomorrow night?"

"Who is Easy?"

"Dad's worker, Carl. His nickname is Easy."

"You want to bring a criminal into our home?"

"He doesn't have a family. I think it would be good for him."

"Well Tommy when you go to jail they don't let you bring a family with you."

"He's not in jail. He's in the halfway house."

"Tommy, the halfway house is like jail. It just doesn't have any bars on the windows."

Mom wiped at the corners of her mouth careful not to smear the bright red lipstick that covered her lips.

"Yeah but."

This was the puzzling part to me about Christianity. My empathy for Easy was stronger than my mother even though she spent most of her free time claiming to be spreading the word of God. I knew when she cut me off mid sentence that Easy would not be sitting at our dinner table, not tomorrow night and not any night.

"Tommy, we'll pray for Carl that he finds a way to let Jesus Christ into his life. If he accepts Jesus then he will be freed of his sins and transgressions."

My mother gave me a look that I have a hard time explaining. It reeked of condescension and snobbery.

"But you don't understand."

My dad had been silent on the subject to this point. Holier than thou was an impossible foe to defeat. He was tired and not about to take on my mother.

"Tommy they don't put people in jail unless they've committed some kind of crime. I have a better idea. Why don't you invite Easy to visit the church on Sunday? If he is truly repentant then he'll embrace a chance to be one of God's children."

"But he didn't sin mom. He was just afraid."

My father felt an impending need to mediate the conversation between my mother and me. He knew that I was waging a losing battle. In my mother's eyes, only a born again Christian was welcomed into heaven.

"Tommy, your mom obviously isn't comfortable having Easy for dinner so let's just leave it at that."

"He sounds like trouble. It's probably not a great idea for you to be spending your days surrounded by criminals."

My mother's face had some kind of weird muscle memory programmed into it that returned her expression to that condescending smile that I just couldn't stand.

"He's not a criminal! He just hasn't had a chance yet to make something of himself."

"Oh please Tommy. They all get chances; they just choose to throw them away. I'm so tired of hearing the sob stories of these savages. You probably didn't know they get to go to college for free if they wanted to huh?"

I sat tight-lipped letting my mother preach from the top of her soapbox.

"Yeah they do. Meanwhile people like us have to break our backs just to get by let alone save money for our children to go to college. Why don't they get off their lazy asses and make something of themselves? They got more opportunities than us white people do and the bottom line is that they're just too lazy to work."

I only needed to say six words to remind my mom of one fatal flaw she had forgotten during her rant against Easy.

"But Easy has a job mom."

"That criminal only has a job because your father took pity on him. He should be grateful he's not rotting in some prison cell."

My mother's temperament was changing. I rarely argued with her as strongly as I did on this night but I felt obligated to step to the defense of Easy, a man she had never met but seemed to know everything about.

"Tommy, your mother has made it clear she's not comfortable with him coming over so we need to let it go."

When my mom was angry the muscles in her body tensed. Her thin neck tightened exposing bulging blood vessels.

The tension between my mother and father seemed to have been growing with each week of the summer. There was a noticeable distance between them. It had started as she became more active with her church this past winter. Religion had a strange effect on my mother. She was less tolerant as she became more involved in her church and now with religion taking up a larger part of her life she was also much more judgmental.

"Tommy, are you finished?"

"Yes ma'am."

"Then put your plate in the sink please and get the clothes off the line."

The debate was over. I stood up from the dinner table and followed her instructions.

I walked to the backyard and began taking the stiffened clothes from the clothesline. My mind wondered what was being said inside the walls of our house. I knew that my parents were no doubt fighting again. To me it seemed senseless. I was trying to do the right thing. I was only trying to welcome someone into our house so that he could be a part of a normal family ritual like eating dinner together.

I took the clothes off the clothesline and slowly folded them. I took my time so that whatever had to be said in the house could be said before I returned. The clothes were stiff when they came off the clothesline, not soft like when they come out of a gas dryer.

It was no big deal folding the clothes but I always felt uncomfortable taking down my mom's bras and underwear. They were as my father called them "Manhattan lingerie". Her bras were red and black just like her underwear and were made out of a shiny silky material. I unclipped them from the line and let them drop into the clothesbasket without touching them and then folded the other clothing and laid them on top to cover the undergarments up.

Inside of our house, I pictured a one-sided conversation that started with my mom following a recipe for salvation that Pastor Jim had brainwashed her with and my father patiently listening but too exhausted to fight back. I now had a measuring stick to compare my own life to. No matter what was being said, I still had it easier than Easy did when he was my age. That's the thing that my mother didn't understand. The person that she was sitting in judgment of had taught me a valuable lesson and had made me appreciate my family more than I ever had before yet he wasn't welcome in our home. If only she could understand the way my father did but she couldn't. Easy wouldn't be coming for dinner that week or any other week and I wouldn't be asking her again.

Chapter 11

Dad had lost the argument with mom by forfeit. He knew that it was futile to debate something that she was so clearly against. There wouldn't be any family dinners with Easy as a guest. It was a battle that my father didn't feel like fighting. He used his time at the work sites to make Easy feel welcome.

Easy was no longer just a day laborer that my father hired. He was a friend. The sultry summer days began to blend into one another for me. Mondays became Tuesdays and Thursdays became Fridays. I lost sense of which day of the week it was. We worked long hours. It was hard physical labor and as I learned how to do more and more of the day to day work, I noticed that my father began spending less time doing the work himself.

He welcomed the break from the physical activity. He had developed a phlegm filled cough that made his lungs sound hollow. The coughing spells would go on for ten or twenty seconds until the phlegm was moved from his throat to his mouth so that he could spit it out.

The coughing spells seemed to drain him of his energy. It was okay though because Easy and I could manage the physical part of the job. We did all of the digging, the hammering and the lifting. Dad arranged the work, ordered the materials, and handled the planning of each job. He seemed to enjoy his newfound role. I don't think he planned it that way but he enjoyed directing us and watching us as we became better and better at what we were doing.

For several weeks now only Easy and I had been accompanying my father to the work sites. The other day laborer was no longer necessary.

In two short months I had learned how to shingle a roof, pour cement, hang sheetrock and frame a wall. I enjoyed all of it. I learned something new everyday and I could see the pride growing inside of my father as he watched his son learn the trade that he loved so much himself.

Easy also had grown not only in his carpentry skills but also as a man. He hadn't missed a workday all summer long. That meant he hadn't been searching the inside of a liquor bottle for answers to his feelings of inadequacy. For Easy, there wasn't any middle ground when it came to drinking. He either drank until he passed out or he didn't drink at all and now that he had exercised some of his internal demons, he didn't have a need to turn to alcohol to soothe his problems.

Our jobs took us all over the county. Dad had even turned over the driving duties to me. He liked not having to drive. I was comfortable driving his truck now. Working the clutch was an afterthought. I drove the truck from dead stops to smooth starts easing the pressure with my foot on and off the clutch pedal. It had taken awhile but now I knew how much pressure to apply, when to pump the gas pedal and when to shift gears.

Dad just told me where to go and when to turn, the rest was up to me.

On the weekends, he had continued taking me to the firing range. I still wasn't much of a marksman but I was beginning to hit more clay pigeons with each passing visit so I knew I was improving.

Now that I had made several visits to the firing range, I had even more respect for dad's ability to hit a whirling clay disc with a shotgun.

He could blast a clay pigeon out of the air as easily as I could shift from first to second gear. It was effortless for dad. He encouraged me and told me that he hadn't become a good shot overnight but I didn't believe him. I saw grown men at the firing range every time we went. Many of them were as old as dad or older and had been shooting a gun just as long as he had but they still struggled with the fleeting gray discs of clay. Dad downplayed his ability but he was special. Even if I could never be as good as dad was I knew that I could be a lot better than I was now.

We went to the firing range each weekend on Sunday afternoon. Dad would coach and I would shoot. I would get discouraged but he would always find something positive to point out to make me feel better. Maybe I wasn't hitting any more clay pigeons but either I was reacting quicker or the gun was steadier as it rested against my shoulder.

We said goodbye to Henry and loaded the shotguns into the pickup. Dad threw me the keys and opened the passenger door.

"You're definitely getting better. Just remember to be patient. Rome wasn't built in a day."

Dad pulled a hanky out of his pants pocket and held it to his mouth as he went through yet another coughing spell. I moved the truck into first gear and pulled out onto the dusty gravel road. When he had finished coughing, he reached into his shirt pocket, lit up a cigarette and rolled down the passenger door window.

It was dusk and the sun was just beginning to set to the west. It sent a brilliant orange and pink glow over the horizon. I wasn't the only one to notice the breathtaking sunset. Dad was enamored also with the colors as he stared across the tops of the cornfields. It was relaxing driving down the country road with the colors from the sunset gently raining down upon the fields in front of us.

Suddenly my father reached his left arm over and held up his hand in front of me.

"Whoa. Slow down there's a deer up here in the ditch."

Dad's vision was amazing. It probably had something to do with why he was such an incredible marksman. I hadn't seen the deer. Even after he had first told me to slow down the deer eluded me. I finally found it on the right hand side of the road standing like a statue. It was a large buck about twenty feet off to the side of the road.

"Pull over", dad directed.

I brought the truck to a stop on the soft dirt shoulder of the road parallel to where the buck had been standing. Our presence had scared him and he had run back into the field still within our vision but out of our reach and a safe distance from the road.

Dad's head made a slow rotation surveying the surrounding area in front of us and to the sides of us. His senses were operating at full capacity

"What is it dad?"

"Shush."

Dad abruptly brought my question to a halt.

"Where there's one deer there are always more."

I looked to either side of me as far as I could see. If there were more deer they had hidden themselves awfully well because I couldn't see them and my vision was perfect.

I followed dad's lead craning my head around and looking for any signs of another deer.

"I don't see any."

Dad had a look of concern. He reached for the door handle and pulled it outward opening the passenger door.

"I know. That's what bothers me."

Dad had grown up around nature his whole life. He knew the area's wildlife and their tendencies and something told him that there was something wrong.

Dad got out of the truck and I followed. The buck held his ground about a hundred feet away on the edge of a cornfield. He snorted and lifted his head up and down. He was statuesque as he stood his eyes fixated on us. I followed dad into the tall grass of the ditch. He stumbled slightly going down the front side of the ditch. He regained his balance and we climbed up the other side of the embankment of the grass to a flat area between the cornfield and the road.

"Keep your eye on that buck."

I laughed off dad's warning and was quickly corrected.

"C'mon, he's afraid of us dad."

"He weighs more than you and I put together. Keep your eyes on him."

Dad was right, where there was one deer near the country roads there would invariably be more.

We edged our way closer to the buck, carefully monitoring whether or not he was preparing to go on the offensive.

"There's something over there. He's not moving because there is something there."

Dad saw some movement in the grass in front of the buck and heard a very faint whimpering sound like an animal in distress. It was subtle but there definitely had been a sound.

Now I knew why the buck hadn't ran further into the field. He was standing guard over a wounded doe that lay in front of him in the deep green grass. The doe was helpless and shaking. Its rear legs were nothing more than bloody pulps of flesh. It was obvious that it had been hit by a car or truck and could make it no further than to where it lay now. Either it had somehow managed to crawl there or the collision with whatever had hit it had thrown it deep into the grass.

If you've ever seen a deer face to face then you've seen the gentle spirit that flows from their eyes. This doe had the biggest darkest eyes I had ever seen on an animal. The sadness and the pain were timidly staring back at our human figures. It wriggled its front legs trying to move in the grass, trying to escape our presence. It was afraid and suffering tremendously. Suddenly the buck took a few sudden steps in our direction and snorted again. I jumped backwards tripping over my own feet and landing on my ass while my father held his ground. The doe lay its head back down in the tall grass submissively as it realized that despite its struggles it was going to be unable to move.

I was panicked. I had never been in a situation like this before. I felt helpless and yet my compassion for the suffering doe begged my inner self to take some action to help.

"What are we going to do dad?"

"Go get me my shotgun and a couple of shells quick!"

"You can't shoot her dad! We have to bring her to a vet."

The buck cautiously moved a few more steps in our direction, as if it was trying to listen in on our conversation.

"Son, this deer is suffering and I mean suffering badly. I know it's not an easy thing to do but we need to relieve her of the misery she is in. That buck is just standing watch over her until she passes on. He's here to make sure no coyotes or scavengers start feeding on her while she's still got a heartbeat."

"Couldn't the vet stitch her up? We can bring her home. I'll take care of her."

"Tommy, if we don't put this deer out of its misery it is just going to linger in the grass until it dies. Sometimes there just isn't anything that a veterinarian can do. I'm sorry but we've got to put it down."

I knew my father was right but I really wanted to save the doe. Dad hated seeing animals suffer. It seems like a contradiction when you're speaking about a man who enjoys hunting pheasants so much but he could see a distinct difference between hunting game that would end up on the dinner table and hunting game only to mount a head and antlers to a living room wall.

Dad kept a steady eye on the buck while I ran back up through the ditch to retrieve his shotgun from behind the seat of our truck. I loaded two shells into it and reversed my tracks. This time as I carried the loaded shotgun I moved more slowly and carefully up and down the grade of the ditch.

I was breathing heavily by the time I reached my father. I handed him the shotgun and took a step backwards.

Dad pumped the shotgun loading a round into the chamber.

I looked again into the eyes of the deer. It was trembling and breathing rapidly. I moved forward and reached my hand down behind its ears and gently stroked the fur on the back of her neck. Her skin was cold to the touch and the fur was dry and not soft like that of a cat or a dog. I had never been this close to a deer before. It was so harmless and innocent as it lay there in the grass. I tried desperately to fight back the tears that I felt welling up in my eyes. I knew it was only a matter of moments before she would draw her last breath.

"Step back Tommy."

I stood back up and got to a position beside my father.

Dad held the shotgun with his right hand and squeezed me around the shoulder with his left hand. I turned my face into his chest and looked up to see that even his eyes were watery.

"Come on Tommy, you're just making this harder on all of us. We're just taking care of the inevitable without making her suffer any longer."

Animals have always amazed me. In one last instinctive and protective manner the large male buck began a slow trot in our direction. Somehow, he sensed what we were about to do. Whether the buck knew the reasoning behind our intentions we'll never know but I think animals are a lot smarter than people give them credit for. They are still God's creatures. They manage to bear their young in the wilderness without the need for a team of doctors and nurses. God has already equipped them with everything that is necessary to continue to procreate their species.

As the buck began to edge closer dad raised his shotgun skyward and pulled the trigger discharging one round in a loud thunderous explosion. The buck turned and ran deep into the cornfield this time. It was a quick bouncy run with dirt clods being kicked loose behind him.

"Take a step back Tommy."

Dad steadied the muzzle of his shotgun about six inches from the chest cavity where the deer's heart was rapidly beating and fired again. As he fired, I turned my head, closed my eyes and gritted my teeth together.

I slowly opened my eyes and turned my head again to face the doe. Her eyes were still open. Still large and black but they were without the same sad expression. She was no longer trembling and her head lay peacefully in the deep green grass. Her suffering had ended and I knew that my father had done the right thing.

Even so I could tell it bothered him to have had to pull the trigger. He had a sullen expression even though he knew it was his duty and the humane thing to do. He nudged the doe gently with the end of his shotgun to make sure she was truly dead and held his hand in front of her nostrils. There was no reflex, no expiration of breath as her chest fell still.

"Take my gun back up to the truck and get the spades from the back of it. We're going to dig a grave so she can rest in peace."

I retreated to the truck and returned with the spades a minute later. These spades were normally reserved for digging holes for fence posts or footings for sidewalks and driveways. This time they served a more important purpose. The dirt was nice and soft despite the cooler temperatures. I did most of the digging. It was a good-sized hole, about five feet deep and several feet wide. I picked her up around her neck and dad grabbed her by the rear quarters as we gently slid her into a shallow blackened grave. We covered her back up with the loose soil and stepped on the dirt packing it firmly to hide her scent and make it more difficult for scavengers like the coyotes that roamed these areas of South Dakota to dig her out.

An hour and a half had passed since we had stopped. We dropped the shovels back into the bed of the truck and got into the cab. I turned the key in the ignition and looked back over my shoulder out the rear window of the truck. Dad was looking straight ahead. The events of the past hour seemed to have left him saddened and unusually quiet.

"Hey dad, look."

Dad turned his head and looked over his right shoulder. The buck that had been keeping watch over his injured mate slowly emerged from the cornfield from which he had disappeared. The buck's eyes were locked on our truck as he cautiously trotted forward, his head slightly lowered. He continued walking until he reached the spot of the freshly dug grave. Then and only then, he took his eyes off us, moved his nose to a position just inches above the dirt sniffing the area where we had just buried the doe. Then in a moment that I will never forget, he laid down directly on top of the grave.

I swallowed hard and my dad turned to me with a look of disbelief.

"Tommy, they're more human than most people will ever understand."

Chapter 12

I moved the truck into first gear and we merged back onto the gravel road, and drove toward our house.

That evening I was lying on my bed, counting up the money I had saved so far that summer. I had over eight hundred dollars already. It was far more than any amount of money I had ever had before. I gathered up the loose bills and put them back into the wooden box that I kept under my bed.

My bedroom door suddenly opened and my mother stood over me as I lay on the bed. She looked at me as if she wanted to question what I was doing but instead she gave me one quick directive.

"Don't forget about church in the morning. I need to be their early so I need you dressed and ready to go by eight."

"Do I have to go?"

"Your father has you five days a week. I don't think it will kill you to spend a few hours with me. Eight o'clock sharp! Got it?"

"Yes ma'am."

I retired early that night. The hard work and long days from the past few weeks had left me exhausted by Saturday evening. Other than reading at night I had little energy left to do much of anything else.

I rode with my mother to the church. Dad wasn't a church member but I was expected to attend. We sat in the second row of the small meeting room. There were two sections of seating all made up of metal folding chairs. Remarkably all of the seats filled in around us. My mother was dressed to the nines including a rather colorful hat and a pair of matching red leather pumps.

In terms of attractive women at the small Pentecostal church we attended my mother had very little competition when it came to the other parishioners. She wasn't the youngest woman in the congregation but she was the classiest in terms of appearance.

My attendance was nothing more than pacification for my mother. I had no interest in being at church and found the antics of Pastor Jim to be less than "Oscar worthy". Other than the subject matter of the sermon that was preached the rest of the performance repeated itself from week to week.

This week's lesson was on "unconditional love". Pastor Jim took center stage with a predictably soft voice that he used to capture the churchgoers attention. They physically leaned forward turning their heads so they wouldn't miss a word he was saying. He used short sentences that grew in volume and intensity to elicit a smattering of "hallelujahs and praise Jesus'".

My mother was entranced when Pastor Jim took the pulpit. Her eyes never left him and she was clearly under what looked like a hypnotic trance.

Pastor Jim stepped down from the small stage and held a bible open in his left hand while his right hand gyrated wildly in a clenched fist.

"So when Christ carried that cross through those muddy streets, with mobs of angry people jeering him and pelting him with stones, he did that for you my brethren. And when those same people placed that thorny crown upon his head, tearing open his skin and causing his blood to spill down the temples of his forehead remember, he did that for you!"

"Amen", an elderly woman in the front row shouted with her fists stretched upward into the air. Pastor Jim dabbed at the sweat that was forming on his forehead with a white clothe handkerchief.

"And when they laid his body on top of that cross, imagine the pain he felt as they pounded those rugged iron spikes that we call nails through his hands and through his feet so that he could be dangled in front of everyone to witness his crucifixion. He did that for whom?"

"Praise Jesus. He did that for us!"

"Amen, Edward Nelson. He did that for you!"

Pastor Jim enunciated each syllable of each word leaving a small theatrical beat in between the words as his sermon began to near a fever pitch. Small balls of spit flew from his lips and he began to sweat profusely. Parishioners stood and swayed with their arms extended upward toward the heavens. Hands held bibles upward toward the stained acoustical tile ceiling while people closed their eyes and some even began to cry. My mother was no exception. She stood and urged me to stand as well, I resisted though. It was bad enough that I was forced to attend a church service each week that I had no interest in but I wasn't about to feign any more interest than I actually had in the events going on around me. Pastor Jim continued to throw gasoline on the spiritual fire that he had burning ignited inside of his congregation.

"When the nail pierced the flesh of his hand, he did that for you Irma Brown and why?"

Irma Brown was an extremely heavyset woman who always sat front and center each week. She stretched herself over two folding chairs and there was little doubt that she had a secret crush on Pastor Jim. It seemed that the ten seconds of acknowledgement from Pastor Jim was enough to keep Irma coming back week after week with those crisp twenty dollar bills she dropped into the offering tray.

"Unconditional love Irma Brown. Say it with me. Unconditional love!"

Irma Brown would be back the next week, the hook had been set and she had received her fifteen seconds of affection.

Pastor Jim then moved back across the front of the stage on the floor below and stopped squarely in front of my mother. I hated this part of Sunday church service, the moment that Pastor Jim interacted with my mother. I had no reason to be embarrassed because everyone in attendance except for me had clearly let go of their inhibitions.

"And Avery Thomsen, as Jesus hung on that cross bleeding, his lips chapped and his tongue thirsty and his feet crippled from the spikes that had been driven through them he did that for you and why? Unconditional love!"

My mother smiled and appeared to blush as Pastor Jim locked into a stare with her that seemed to last well a lot longer than the ten seconds that it lasted.

Pastor Jim moved back atop the stage and stood in front of his pulpit and like any skilled thespian he lowered the volume of his voice forcing the parishioners to listen intently and position themselves to lean in ever so slightly closer to the place where he stood. In hushed tones he continued speaking to the congregation. I looked at the clock. Thank God I thought to myself. Only a few more minutes and the service should be over.

Pastor Jim stood with both hands on the pulpit. His face was reddened and sweat now poured freely across his forehead and down his face.

"He hung on that cross bleeding to death as the sun beat upon him with nary a cloud in the sky blocking its rays because God promised unconditional love to you and each of your children. And you ask yourselves, Pastor Jim what do I have to do to receive this generous gift from our heavenly father? What?"

Pastor Jim then slammed his hand on the pulpit causing a simultaneous jerk among the congregation as he caught them off guard with the loud bang created by his hand slapping the hard oak front of the pulpit.

"Seek forgiveness for your sins my children. That's all", Pastor Jim said in his softest tone yet.

I had the formula for Pastor Jim's sermons figured out. That was his "Perry Mason" moment for the congregation. That was the message that they were supposed to leave the church with that day that kept them in a state of awe and contemplation until the following week. Then we would see the same performance play itself out within the same walls of this church with a slightly different message.

"Can I hear an Amen?"

The congregation on cue said a voluminous "Amen" including my mother who may have said it louder than any other person who was there.

I embarrassedly looked at my mother who wiped away tears from the corners of her eyes and looked down on me with a smile as large as Pastor Jim's ego.

"Would everyone please turn their hymnals to page 53 and join me as we sing, The Old Rugged Cross".

Pages rustled in a dozen worn out hymnals and my mother held hers firmly in front of her anxiously awaiting Doris to play the intro to the song on the church organ.

"Doris", Pastor Jim said loudly cuing the start of the song.

As soon as the hymn ended Pastor Jim greeted each church member near the front door. I stood a step behind my mother with what I would assume was a disinterested look frozen to my face.

"Avery. Tommy". Pastor Jim's teeth seemed extra white this morning for some unknown reason.

"Did I see you leading the congregation in song today Tommy?"

"No sir", I politely replied. My mother flashed a fake smile and chuckled with some insincere laughter.

"Well I could swear I saw your lips moving."

"Yes sir, I fake it. I move my lips so the people around me think I'm singing".

"I love a boy with a sense of humor", Pastor Jim cackled with little sincerity.

Pastor Jim reached his hand forward to rest it on my shoulder and I reflexively slid my shoulder just out of his reach.

"Mom, can I run over to the bookstore?"

"Make it snappy", my mother said rather unenthusiastically.

The part I enjoyed most about Sunday church service was running across the street to the used bookstore. Sometimes I would get lucky and there would be two or three books that I hadn't read but either way it got me away from the church and Pastor Jim.

Angelino's Used Books was one of the few stores open for business on Sunday. I worked my way to the soft cover fiction, hoping to find a Doc Savage novel that I hadn't yet read.

"I thought you were saving your money for a car?"

The voice startled me. I spun around to find Easy standing behind me.

"What are you doing here", I asked smiling.

"I saw you come in and thought I'd say hello. Have you ever read any books by Zane Grey?"

Easy holds up a western novel titled, "Heritage of the Desert".

"No, I'm not much into westerns."

"He's a good writer. You should read him some time. So where's your old man", Easy asked.

"He's at home. My mom drags me to church every Sunday over there."

Easy and I stood at the front window glass of Angelino's Used Books and looked across the street to the church.

"Is that your mom in the red shoes," Easy asked rather surprised.

"Yeah, that's the Jesus freak", I responded.

"She's a pretty lady."

"Yeah, I guess. It's kind of hard to think of your mom like that."

"Who's the dude with the fancy suit?"

"That's Pastor Jim", I snickered.

We watched as Pastor Jim and my mother were engaged in what appeared to be a rather light hearted conversation. Each of them took turns breaking into spontaneous laughter when the other ceased speaking.

"Apparently, Pastor Jim is a pretty funny guy?"

"He's a phony. I can't stand the guy."

Easy and I continued to watch my mother and Pastor Jim converse. My mom moved forward and appeared to brush some lint from the shoulder of Pastor Jim's suit jacket.

"Well, I better get going," I told Easy.

I reached into my front pocket and grabbed some change to pay for the book I had found. Easy grabbed my forearm before it could reach the payment counter with the loose change I held in my hand.

"Forget about it. This book is on me."

"Thanks Easy".

I turned and walked to the exit door and then stopped.

"If you ever feel the urge, I'm stuck over there every Sunday. You know what they say, misery loves company".

Easy gave me a big smile.

"You never know. Maybe I'll surprise you one day. See you tomorrow buddy".

I walked back across the street to where my mother and Pastor Jim were standing. I timed my trip to the bookstore well as they were finishing up their small talk.

My mother and I got back into the green Plymouth and began driving back to our house. We didn't converse while driving like my father and I did, mostly because I didn't have much to say to my mother. We had really grown in opposite directions, especially over the past year. Dad and I could talk about cars, work or guns and never run out of things to say to each other. My mother and I however had very little in common anymore. I couldn't carry on any kind of intelligent conversation that dealt with religion and that was my mother's one topic of interest so instead I began reading the used book I had just picked up.

On this day my mother caught me off guard. She usually never spoke so long as I was sitting quietly across the bench seat from her.

"You probably don't realize how important going to church is for me. You've got your books and your father has his business and I have church. That's my escape from boredom and routine. I know you're not interested in it the same way as I am but this is my outlet from everyday life."

It was an odd and unexpected dialogue from my mother but apparently she wanted me to understand how important church was to her.

"You remember that next time you embarrass me by telling the Pastor that you just pretend you're singing by moving your lips. Why do have such disdain for him? He's done nothing to you and when he tries to make small talk you act like there's a fire underneath your feet and you can't get away from him fast enough. I don't understand Tommy but regardless you need to respect my friends. I don't want to have to talk about this again. Do you understand?"

"Yes ma'am."

I've learned a lot from my father this summer both from what he's shown me and from what I've watched him do when he didn't know I was paying attention. I learned not to argue with my mother when it was a losing battle. I could have given her a laundry list of the reasons why I didn't like Pastor Jim but it would have only created unneeded tension and in the end I would be no closer to convincing her that he wasn't the person that she wanted to believe he was. I had my instincts and I trusted them. I would pacify mom by going to church with her but that's as far as my interest in the church would ever extend.

We sat side by side in the Plymouth and said nothing further the rest of the ride. I returned to my book and my mother returned to the thoughts that were playing inside of her head.

Chapter 13

Easy and I continued to carry the brunt of the workload as my father's cold worsened. His coughing spells were more frequent and were lasting longer.

"Hey Bob, maybe you should get that checked out. They can probably give you something so you don't end up with pneumonia."

It was the first time Easy had mentioned a concern about my father's cough.

I knew the word pneumonia. That is what had eventually cost my grandmother her life. Of course, she was a lot older than my dad when pneumonia brought her to the hospital.

She too had a terrible cough that was unrelenting and lasted for several days before my uncles took her to see a doctor.

"I'm tougher than you think Easy. Don't worry about me", my father said with a smile."

Dad rarely visited the doctor's office with the exception of visits brought on by stitches and splints. In fact, I can hardly remember a time when he had so much as the flu or a runny nose even with the unrelenting winters and damp spring weather of South Dakota. Dad said the way to beat a bug was by telling your mind repeatedly that you refuse to be sick. He felt the mind was the most powerful organ in the human body. The mind to him was stronger than any medicine that a doctor could prescribe and certainly stronger than any virus. His shear willpower had kept him in a strong and healthy condition for as long as I had been around.

Easy and I became a good team. Dad was there to answer our questions and offer us guidance. Until he felt better, he had opted to take a break from the physical labor. He would sit on the tailgate of the truck at the work site and smoke as he watched us work. He became increasingly comfortable with our work as we made less and less mistakes and had fewer questions to ask.

Easy it turned out was a natural when it came to carpentry. He had a real knack for the craft. Without the guidance of my father, he may have never had the opportunity to learn that about himself. I had the feeling that my father was as proud of Easy as he was of me. Easy in many ways was a part of our family. He was there to earn a paycheck but more importantly, he had a purpose in his life that had been missing the first nineteen years of his existence.

Chapter 14

Sunday's were our only day off from work during the summer. Weather kept my father limited on the days he could work during the winter so while the weather was warm he took on as many jobs as possible.

My mother on the other hand spent Sunday mornings at church attending services and teaching Sunday school to the adults. I was forced to go with her most weeks but occasionally I was able to weasel my way out of going along. My father would usually catch up on things around the house or work on the truck. I had the day to myself. I would go fishing or get lost in a world of make believe also known as a book.

I had told my father I was going to spend the afternoon fishing at the creek behind our house but I changed my mind. I started reading a new Doc Savage adventure novel that morning and I was hooked. I couldn't leave to go fishing now. I had to know that Doc would be safe and that his gang of geniuses would live to fight another day. The only way to find out was to read on and see how they would overcome the evil force that they were up against this time. I lounged on my bed with book in hand and quickly traveled to a faraway place where nothing was impossible. I stayed there for a couple of hours turning page after page until I heard a car crunching the gravel on our driveway. I sat up and looked out the window. I pulled the curtains aside just enough to get a clear view of the driveway.

It was that afternoon that I learned firsthand how a person's life can be turned upside down in an instant. Much like the night when Easy took matters into his own hands with a baseball bat the course of his life was forever changed. In a single moment he changed the path that his life would follow. He hadn't planned to send his life in a different direction when he woke up that morning and I hadn't planned on my life taking the direction that it was about to take when I rose this morning either.

I was about to share in an unplanned moment that would change the course of my own life. When I woke up it had felt like any other Sunday. Nothing was out of the ordinary really; it was just a lazy afternoon. Now a few hours later life was about to deliver a kick to the stomach that would knock the wind out of me and leave me on my back gasping for air.

The car in the driveway belonged to my Aunt Gloria, Tommy's widow. She had driven the roughly one hundred miles to visit with my dad. There was nothing unusual about this. She would drive to our house to visit with my father regularly. My father and Gloria had bonded ever since Uncle Tommy's tragic accident.

Dad walked out of the garage to greet her. They had a short but intense conversation. There faces were painted with serious demeanors. Gloria gave my father a tight hug before walking with him toward the house with her arm around his waist. I ducked my head away from the window instinctively. For some reason I felt like this was intended to be a private moment and I was somehow intruding upon it.

The front screen door creaked on its hinges as the rusty spring that held it to the doorframe stretched wide open. Suddenly the make believe world I had escaped to was shattered.

I heard sobbing sounds coming from outside of my door. It was my aunt and my father in conversation and my father crying as he spoke. He and Gloria were in the living room and she was consoling him as he spoke.

"Are you sure we're alone?"

My Aunt Gloria's voice cracked as she asked the question.

"Avery is at church and Tommy went up to the creek to go fishing."

My father and Aunt were barely audible. I needed to move closer to the inside of my bedroom door in order to hear their conversation clearly. I sat the book down on my bed. The springs inside of the mattress quietly squeaked as I shifted my weight from the bed to the floor.

I walked quietly to my partially open bedroom door and stopped. That's as close as I could get to the living room without being discovered. I wasn't supposed to be in the house that afternoon. I wasn't supposed to hear the private conversation that my father and Gloria were having. I hadn't intended to mislead my father into thinking I wasn't in the house. I was paralyzed with fear and shock. I was fourteen years old and this was the first time I had ever heard my father cry. I needed to know why. Something had to be horribly wrong in order to bring my father to tears. Thoughts raced through my head. Maybe someone he loved had died. Maybe something happened to Easy. I had to know what it was that had brought him to tears.

It's not that my father was without emotion it's just that he was so strong. He had no problem displaying love or anger. Those emotions I had seen on many occasions. Some people might call him guarded. He was careful to never show a moment of weakness. I guess crying would have been contrary to the battle tested larger than life image that he had always projected to me and everyone else. In my eyes, my father was Doc Savage. He was a mighty, strong and impenetrable human fortress. There was no kryptonite on the planet that could stop my dad until I heard Gloria and him speaking.

They began discussing an evil and ugly word that I was about to become more familiar with than I had ever desired.

I continued to stand behind the door cautiously listening to the conversation that was taking place in the living room.

A sinking feeling overcame me like nothing I had ever experienced before. This moment felt closer to fiction than the book I had been reading. I had no idea of my father's illness. I had heard the cough get progressively worse. I had seen him shy away from the physical work that he had done before so effortlessly. Neither of these things caused me any concern. I believed as he had told me that he was simply battling a summer cold that had gripped him and was stubbornly hanging on.

As I listened however, I learned that weeks had gone by with cancer living inside of him yet he had never said a word to me about it.

He told my aunt that he didn't want me to worry needlessly. There was nothing that I could do to stop the illness from progressing. It would have been as futile as trying to extinguish a forest fire a teaspoon of water at a time.

His prognosis was bleak. The disease had spread into several vital organs and he used the word terminal more than once while speaking with my aunt. My skin felt cold and clammy.

This was unchartered territory for me. Hopelessness was never a part of the vocabulary I had been taught but the more I listened the more hopeless I felt. Faith had always been a fixture of my father's determination and strength. He would get better, wouldn't he? He had to. I mean after this was no ordinary person this was my father and he was my superhero and everyone knows that superheroes are invincible! Just like in the many books that I had read, the superhero always prevails.

Doc Savage always found a way out of the situations he was in even if it seemed as if there was no possible way to escape. Somehow he would still find a way to overcome the obstacle he was facing. Doc would fight and plot and then through a combination of strength, wit and determination, he would triumph.

Why couldn't my father's story have the same miraculous ending as the dozens of novels I had read? I had been taught my whole life that good overcomes evil. In church I was taught to believe that goodness would prevail. On television the guys in the black hats always ended up surrendering to the guys in the white hats.

This however wasn't a used book and this wasn't a television show. This was a reality that was immediately sobering, like accidentally touching your finger on a hot iron. You jerk your hand away from the iron but you have already burned your skin. Proof of the hot iron is left behind in the form of a throbbing pain and a blister. You can't go back and rewrite that previous moment. Once your skin makes contact with the red-hot surface of that iron, the page has already been written.

If what my father was telling my aunt was true then my father's story was going to have a very different ending than any of the Doc Savage novels I had read. That became more and more apparent as I eavesdropped to him as he gave the morbid details of the disease to my aunt.

I felt horrible, not just because of the devastating news about my father but also because of the way I had learned about it. I felt as if I had done something morally wrong by listening in on his private conversation. A combination of guilt, sadness and shock all overwhelmed me at the same time.

I peeked through the half-inch crack between the doorframe and the door. My aunt sat in front of my father holding his hands as he spoke. The fact that tears had been shed was all I needed to see to understand the seriousness of the situation. From where I stood I could hear every word clearly. It was eavesdropping, but I had to know every detail.

"It's in my liver", my father said as my aunt's shoulders sagged.

"What can they do? There has to be something that they can do."

Gloria was twice my age but equally as naïve as myself when it came to the disease. She was reaching, grabbing desperately for a strand of hope but her fingers kept coming back empty.

"No. There's no cure. There's no magic pill and there is no operation that can help. It's a very aggressive form of cancer."

"What about chemotherapy or radiation?"

My aunt introduced two additional words to my vocabulary that I knew nothing about. She was apparently more educated on this subject than I realized.

"It has spread too far and this type of cancer doesn't respond well to treatment anyway. They would just make me sick and take away the little bit of natural resistance that my body has left.

Dad rubbed at his eyes and tried to compose himself.

"I'm afraid."

I could see my father's hands trembling.

"Not for me, I'm afraid for Tommy. The kid's only fourteen."

He sobbed loudly. His body shook. A lifetime of tears that had been held back found their way out of his eyes. Gloria leaned forward hugging him, looking out over his right shoulder to the paneled wall behind him and focusing on a knot in the wood of the dark walnut paneling.

They held their hug tightly. Dad's eyes closed and the full weight of his body was resting against her petite frame.

I was numb. My legs began shaking. I slumped to the floor accidentally hitting the door with my arm on the way down.

The sound of the crying stopped as suddenly as it had started. My dad cleared his throat and then called out my name.

"Tommy, is that you?"

I sat perfectly still, frozen in complete silence not knowing what to do next. The only thing I did know is that I did not want my dad to find out that I had heard or seen anything.

"You said he's fishing up at the creek."

My dad wanted to make sure. I moved myself quietly on my hands and knees. I crawled across the floor and quickly slid my body under the box spring of my bed. I heard footsteps stop outside my bedroom door. I could see the bottom of the door swinging into my room as he gently pushed the door open.

"Tommy?"

I said nothing. Dad's size thirteen boots were pressed against the carpet only a few feet from where I was lying. The boots were unmistakable; dark brown, snub-nosed and heavily worn. He stepped slowly around my bed and looked around. There was little furniture in my bedroom. It consisted of only a chest of drawers, my twin bed and a card table that served as a makeshift desk.

He walked to the closet door and slid it open. My first instinct had been to hide in the closet. Thank God I had not hid in there. He found it empty and slid the door closed. He walked around to the other side of the bed and sat down.

I quietly turned my head the other direction. It was close quarters and I was feeling a bit claustrophobic. I could see a large brown spider slowly walking along the baseboard of the wall a few inches from my head. I was scared to death of spiders but I ignored it and it quickly disappeared behind the heat vent in the wall. The carpet was itchy on my face. I carefully moved my right hand to my nose and scratched it.

My aunt walked in and sat on the bed beside my father. There were only a few inches between my face and the box spring.

"See, he's out fishing", my aunt said soothingly.

"He's a tough kid Gloria but he's still just a kid."

She reached up with her left hand and caressed my father's back in a circular motion.

"How do you tell your son that you're dying? How do you tell your son that you only have a few more months to share with him?"

"He's going to be okay. So many people care about him. He won't ever be alone."

She placed his right hand in between her own hands and pressed it against her cheek.

"You're a great father. The best any child could ever ask for. He has so many great memories. Those memories will last a lifetime."

My aunt was trying desperately to comfort my father. Her words were reassuring and seemed to help my father regain his composure.

Dad reached to his left and picked up the book I had been reading from the quilt it was lying on. He looked closely at the picture on the front of it. The book cover was a green color and featured a sketch of a muscular Doc Savage balancing himself on a log in the middle of a foggy night in front of an old wooden ship.

"Who is that?"

My father smiled. He had seen me lounging on my bed many times holding one of the soft cover books.

"That's his hero, Doc Savage."

Dad was smart. He was the smartest man I had ever known. He was nearly always right, however this time he was wrong. My hero was sitting above me on my bed. Doc Savage was merely an escape.

Chapter 15

I waited under the bed even after my dad and aunt left the bedroom. I had no choice but to remain silently hidden in my bedroom until she had left. When I heard them leave the house I slid out from under the bed and peaked through the bedroom curtains. Gloria was sitting in her car with my father leaning over the passenger side door. The window was rolled down and his elbows were resting on the window frame.

I knew a conversation was taking place but now I couldn't hear the sounds of their voices let alone the words. My father stood up and my aunt waved to him as she backed the car around so she could turn onto our driveway. My father waved goodbye then walked slowly back to the front porch, sat down on a chair and lit a cigarette.

I carefully climbed out of my bedroom window and hid out of his view. I peaked around the corner of the house making sure that I had a clear path to run behind the house to dad's workshop. There I could grab my fishing pole and tackle box and carry out the rest of my charade.

I made plenty of noise announcing my arrival to dad as I came up the side of the house holding the fishing rod and my small blue tackle box.

"You're back already", my father said in a composed voice.

"They weren't biting."

"You just missed your aunt. She's headed back to Cedar Springs now."

"Is that reel still giving you trouble?"

I looked down to my fishing reel to see a tangled mess of fishing line. If you're not in the practice of lying, it doesn't come easily to you. I've never had to lie, especially to my parents. I was going to have to learn to lie and learn to lie quickly.

"It looks like you had the same problem as the last time you and I went out."

I had forgotten about my fishing reel. I hadn't fixed it since the last fishing trip that my father and I had taken. Even though I wasn't accustomed to lying, I found that I was rather good at it that afternoon. Without a moment of hesitation, the words spilled from my mouth.

"Yeah, it was working fine and then the same thing happened."

I stuttered a bit but then I pulled myself together.

"Between that and the fish not biting it wasn't any fun out there."

Dad seemed satisfied with my answer. I sat the fishing pole and tackle box down in the corner of the porch.

"Dad can I borrow the truck and drive up to the hardware store? I want to get a new reel. This one is a pain in the neck."

"Here, you'll need some money."

Dad reached into his back pocket and pulled out his black leather wallet.

"No I have money in my room."

"Just take the money and quit arguing."

I took a wrinkled twenty-dollar bill from my dad's fingers. I swallowed hard in order to maintain my composure.

"The keys should be in the ignition."

I didn't want a new fishing rod; I wanted to talk to my mother. I had to find out if she knew about the cancer. Was dad keeping it a secret from her too? It was Sunday so it wouldn't be hard to find her.

I walked to the door of the truck and lifted myself onto the driver's seat. Dad watched me from the porch as I settled into position pulling a lever on the side of the seat to move it forward so I could reach the gas and brake pedal more easily. I faked a smile and waved. I put the truck into reverse and backed it away from the garage. Dad jumped up from his seat on the porch and began waving his hands in the air back and forth signaling me to stop the truck. I quickly began praying a silent prayer to myself. God please don't let him ask to come along.

Dad walked to the driver's door window.

"Buckle your seatbelt and keep it under sixty okay?"

"Of course."

I drove forward and exhaled deeply. I had done it. I had made it past my father. Now I had to find a way to ask my mom what she knew. It was late enough that church service would be finished but she had told me the night before that she would be staying late on Sunday getting ready for some fall celebration that was coming soon.

I sped down the gravel road toward County Road 86. I couldn't get to Main Street in Lake Mills quickly enough. My leg shook each time I pushed in the clutch to shift. Never in my life had I been so nervous. Never in my life had I dreamed that a moment like this would find its way into my world.

Chapter 16

I turned right on Main Street and saw our green Plymouth sedan parked in front of the church. It was an immediate sense of relief. I parked the pickup alongside of the curb and shoved it into first gear. I jumped out of the cab and ran to the front door.

The church was an old brick building and a fixture on Main Street for as long as there had been a town of Lake Mills. Originally, the building was a furniture store, a giant open showroom with a glass storefront. The building had been empty for several years until someone had the idea of turning it into a church. The clear glass windows had been replaced with beautiful pieces of stained glass but otherwise the building had remained mostly the same. Folding chairs lined the inside of what had once been the furniture showroom and at the far end of the building stood a small makeshift podium and organ.

I grabbed the door handle twisting my hand back and forth the door was locked. The church services were over so anybody left in the building was probably working in the back in the business office. I remembered that there was a door at the rear of the building. I ran around the corner of the church to the backside of the building. Pastor Jim's Cadillac was parked on a weed ridden gravel alley that ran behind the building.

Pastor Jim's Cadillac was unmistakable in a small town like Lake Mills. The car like Pastor Jim was always perfectly manicured. The whites of his white wall tires were bright and vibrant. The dark black paint had been accented with glistening chrome trim, chrome bumpers and shiny chrome hubcaps. There were no water spots, just the glassy smooth jet-black painted finish. It was a microcosm of the man who drove it. Even the trunk bore the signature of Pastor Jim. In large gold four-inch tall letters it read, "Have You Been Saved?" A finishing touch that was nearly as obnoxious as the neckties that Pastor Jim donned every Sunday.

I made my way to the door of the rear entrance. Perhaps it would be unlocked. I ran up the cement steps, placed my hand on the doorknob and turned it a half turn. The door was unlocked but it was stuck, the wooden door had swollen from the summer's humid air and it now filled every inch of the doorframe that was hinging it. I pushed on the door again but this time I used my shoulder as a human battering ram. The door swung open making a popping noise as it squeezed out of the weather tightened doorframe.

"Mom", I yelled.

I was at the rear of the chapel. Mom usually spent her time after service on the other side of the church, near the business office. I walked hurriedly past the folding chairs yelling for my mother as I moved forward. I turned to the right and made a few steps down the hall that led to the business office.

Pastor Jim stepped into the hall from a doorway. He wasn't wearing his usual three-piece suit that he wore every Sunday. He had on only a dress shirt and a pair of dress slacks. The first two buttons of his dress shirt were unbuttoned and the necktie he was wearing was loose and hanging sloppily in front of him.

"Tommy."

The surprise of seeing me came through in the din of Pastor Jim's voice.

"Pastor Jim I need to talk to my mom right away", I said as I jogged down the hallway.

"Well I'm sorry Tommy but she's not here at the moment. She went up to the grab some dinner for us. What's the matter, maybe I can help?"

"No, I need to talk to her."

The usually silver tongued pastor tripped over his words.

"Uh well why don't you wait here? I'm, uh, sure she'll be back anytime."

I sat down on a folding chair. Pastor Jim was unusually attentive and overly nervous. I was nervous myself. He was stumbling over his words the same way I had tripped over my words when I had lied to my father earlier.

I wiped the sweat away from my forehead with the back of my hand. I looked at Pastor Jim. He was rather unsettled looking. His eyes were darting back and forth between where I was standing and the hallway that led to the business office. Then it dawned on me. Mom's car had been parked in front of the church when I parked the truck.

"How did my mom go to get food? I saw her car parked in front of the church."

"You don't think I'd send her on an errand in that old green Plymouth on a day like this, do you? The air conditioner doesn't work in that old car so I sent her in my Cadillac."

Pastor Jim smiled widely. He was trying to sell me a line of bullshit and now I knew it. He chuckled and tilted his head the other direction. He thought he had fooled me so I smiled back hoping to relax him enough so that he would let his guard down. He chuckled loudly. Then in one quick and fluid motion I darted through a space between him and the wall to his left.

"Tommy, wait."

I ran down the hallway to his office. The door was open and I looked inside.

"Mom, are you here?"

There was no answer and the room was empty except for a desk that was wildly stacked with papers and two large bookcases that stood against the wall. Pastor Jim's suit jacket was hanging over the back of a chair. It was a musty smelling and poorly lighted room.

Pastor Jim walked up behind me and squeezed between me and the messy room. He put his hand on the doorframe as he sweated profusely. The body language told me that he didn't want me to get into his office.

"Tommy, now I told you that your mother went to get us food. You can't come into the house of God and disrespect me like this.

My heart was pounding. I couldn't help myself; my nerves had got the best of me.

"You know what Pastor Jim, you're a phony. No, I take that back. You know what you are? You're a Goddamn liar! Your car is parked behind the church in the alley. I saw it before I came in the back door. I may be younger than you but I'm not an idiot. Where in the hell is my mom?"

Pastor Jim's body was visibly shaking. His frustration was growing and so was the volume of his voice. His face began to redden and now he wagged his pointer finger as he spoke.

"I'm going to tell you for the last time, she went up to the café to get us dinner."

Pastor Jim's eyes darted from me to inside of his office nervously. He was a fool. His body language told me that he didn't want me snooping around his office.

Just then as Pastor Jim and I were on the edge of a full fledged argument my mother stepped out of the lady's restroom just fifteen feet up the hall from where we stood.

"Mom."

"Tommy what's all the screaming about?"

Pastor Jim said you went up to the café to get dinner but both your cars were here when I got here."

"I must have got here right before you Tommy. I came in through the back door and left his car in the alley. He probably never even saw me come in."

Mom was calm but she was in somewhat of disarray. Her hair was out of place slightly and her makeup wasn't applied to her skin in the perfect way that it usually was. Her lips were absent of the sassy red gloss that normally accompanied them. Her attention also kept drifting between me and the interior of Pastor Jim's office. If mom was lying to me then she was a seasoned liar, someone who had spent a lot of time practicing. Other than her eye movement, she was very convincing.

"Jim your sandwich is in the bag on the credenza."

Her voice was smooth and tranquil but her eye contact continued to wander between myself and the desk in Pastor Jim's office.

"Why don't you believe Pastor Jim? Why would he make something like that up Tommy?"

"I need to talk to you in private mom."

My mother pushed past Pastor Jim and I into his office. Pastor Jim walked in to get the brown paper bag that contained his dinner. I wasn't about to say anything until he had left the room and the door was closed. As Pastor Jim picked up his brown paper bag I noticed a piece of red fabric sticking out from underneath a newspaper on his desk. Not a normal piece of fabric either. I recognized it from all the times I had hung laundry at our house. I reached forward, grabbed the end of it and jerked it out revealing one of my mother's lacy red brassieres. Silence permeated the office. I shook my head in disgust. Pastor Jim laid the brown bag back down on the credenza.

"Now wait just one minute Tommy, it's not what you think." Pastor Jim blurted out.

"How the hell do you know what I'm thinking?"

I instinctively grabbed Pastor Jim by his polyester shirt and threw him to the floor. I was a boy and he was a man but none of that mattered right now. I was on my knees kneeling over him. I felt my right hand tightening into a fist. I used my left hand to grip Pastor Jim around the throat pinning him tightly to the ground. My right hand was high above his face clenched tightly into a fist and my arm was shaking just as my legs had been shaking during the drive to the church. He looked at me with a sense of fear streaming from his eyes.

I could smash his face in right now and he knew it. I could feel the pulse of my heart beating inside of my sweaty shirt. The blood that rushed to my face made me warm. My mom stood by helplessly frozen. She finally spoke just as I was ready to unleash my fury.

"Tommy don't do it! If you want to be angry then be angry with me. It's my fault."

My arm quivered and my knuckles were white from my firmly clenched fingers. I wanted so badly to hit him. I wanted to knock each of his pretty, white teeth out. He had a cowardly look on his face. My arm felt like a tightly wound catapult. I thought it might tear itself right out of my shoulder socket as I held it in the air. A rush of energy was swirling within me. It seemed as if minutes had passed since I pinned him to the ground.

My left hand lifted Pastor Jim's head as it held firmly onto his throat and then I reluctantly released my grip, dropping Pastor Jims' head back against the concrete floor. He put his hands to his throat gasping for air. I stood up and looked my mother straight in the eye.

"This is your fault."

My mom burst into tears and wilted to the floor like an untended flower. I walked back down the church hallway. Her sobs grew louder and then softer as I made my way out of the church. I kicked the back door and it swung open forcefully. I grabbed my hair in my hands as I was overcome with sadness. Tears of anger and tears of frustration worked together as a stream of salt water ran down the sides of my cheeks.

I stood on the church steps, trying to compose myself, trying desperately to keep my body from shaking. I wiped at my eyes with the back of my hand and there in the alley behind the church Pastor Jim's Cadillac came into clear focus.

I looked around the ground near my feet and saw a solitary red brick with bits of cracked mortar stuck to it lying in a flowerbed. I picked it up. My heart pumped faster with each footstep I made toward his prized possession. Like moments earlier, I raised my arm high above my head only this time I held the brick in my fist. Consequences were the furthest thing from my mind and this time my emotions got the best of me. I sent the brick crashing into the window. It made a dent in the center of the windshield three inches deep. "

"Piss on them. They deserve each other", I said aloud.

Throwing the brick helped to relieve some of the anger. I bent at the waste and took several deep breaths. My body was slowly coming under control.

"Tommy!"

I turned to see my mother. She stumbled clumsily toward me in her high-heeled shoes.

"I don't care and I don't want to hear your excuses."

"There's more to this than you know. It's not what you think", my mother pleaded.

I ignored my mom as I continued my way around the corner of the church toward Main Street where the truck was still parked.

"Tommy, please! Tommy I'm talking to you!"

My mom was so desperate to stop me, so desperate for me to acknowledge her.

"Tommy, you're father is dying."

I stopped and turned to face her. My voice was angry and shaky.

"I know", I growled through my clenched teeth.

I leaned against the door of the truck. Mom stared at me with a look of shock as her mouth hung open in disbelief.

"You know? How do you know?"

My mother had a look of bewilderment and confusion on her face as she asked me the questions.

"I heard him today at the house talking to Aunt Gloria."

"Tommy, you're father swore me to secrecy. I swear to God I wanted to tell you but he didn't want me to."

"You swear to God? That's funny." I shook my head as I climbed back into the truck and started the engine.

My mother quickly followed me to the driver's window stumbling over her own feet as she raced to catch up with me.

"Where are you going?"

"I need to talk to him."

"Please Tommy don't tell your father about Pastor Jim."

"Do you think I give two squirts of piss about Pastor Jim right now?

"I'm afraid Tommy. I've never been alone. I went straight from my parent's house to your father's arms. I didn't know who else to turn to."

"You didn't know who else to turn to?" I parroted. Well, apparently you forgot about me."

I jammed the shifter into first gear and spun the tires on the loose dirt and gravel that was underneath of them causing them to squeal against the pavement as the truck lurched forward wildly. I watched in the rear view mirror as the pathetic image of my mother faded. She stood helplessly with her hands at her sides.

My entire universe had been shattered in one brief afternoon. First finding out that my father was living out a death sentence and then discovering that my once flawless mother was committing the ultimate act of betrayal on my father at the time when he needed her more than any time before.

It would be a lot for any adult to absorb in one afternoon, it was overwhelming for a fourteen year old to digest.

I drove out onto the open highway and pressed the gas pedal to the floorboard. I was commandeering a two ton battering ram and anyone who dared to get in front of my path was in danger. One giant thought quickly replaced all of the other thoughts that had bouncing back and forth inside of my head. Someone else needed to feel the pain that I was feeling. Whether they were deserving recipients or not didn't matter to me.

I had never felt rage like this before. I had heard urban legends of people who developed superhuman strength when a loved one was pinned underneath of a car or trapped inside of a burning building and I imagined that they must have been feeling the same intense rush of energy that I was feeling right now. I dared someone to cross my path in there car. I begged God to put someone in front of me on the road. I would exercise the demons that were pressing against the inside of my skin to get out with one furious explosion of steel and flesh if anyone were to cross my path. Maybe this is how Easy felt right before he lifted the baseball bat and bashed that son of a bitch he called a foster dad across the teeth. If he felt like I did on the inside right now then I knew clearly now why he did what he did. He might have been saving his brother from an unnecessary whipping but the true motivator would have been transferring the anger that was boiling inside of him from months of torture and pain into a stream of energy that vibrated along the barrel of the bat he had held in his hands.

Ahead of me coming down the hill I saw my opportunity to rid my body of the pain. A cattle truck was coming over the hilltop and trying to pass a grain truck that was clogging his lane. They were both moving slowly and I could see that the grain truck was struggling to pass.

I pressed my foot against the gas pedal as tightly as I could press it. I leaned forward over the steering wheel as if my posture would create acceleration. I snarled through gritted teeth and my fingers squeezed the hard surface of the steering wheel.

The cattle truck flashed his lights off and on at me assuming that I hadn't noticed the danger that lay ahead. I let out a primal scream that started somewhere deep inside of my guts and then growled out of my throat. My neck tightened and tears of anger were squeezed from the corners of my eyes.

The cattle truck flashed its lights again off and on three times desperately trying to catch my attention. The pain that I felt would be over in seconds and the families of the asshole in the cattle truck could inherit it from me. It was selfish but I guess that is why they call it blind rage. I couldn't see anything else accept a sudden end to the anxiety that was causing my heart to beat so harshly that it felt like my chest was about to explode. A devilish laughter took over the growl as I still gritted my teeth and then the blasting of the oncoming truck's horn could be heard. The sound of the horn was quickly joined in a disjointed harmony by the shredding of rubber as the grain truck locked his brakes and the cattle truck swerved madly to the right.

The front fender of my truck missed the front of his truck by a fraction of a second and the time stood still for a moment as I witnessed the look of terror and anguish that was frozen on the driver's face.

I screamed by him doing eighty miles an hour. I wondered if he had seen the equally crazy look that I was wearing on my face. I screamed and howled like a wild animal that had just finished a kill. I bounced up and down on the seat of the truck as it cut through the thick nighttime air. My fists pounded up and down on the steering wheel trying to break it or bend it in vain and then finally like a dam that had been holding back a wall of water my turmoil broke through in a flood of tears and uncontrollable sobbing. My foot slowly eased up on the gas pedal and I shifted the truck into neutral as I coasted along the deserted highway until it slowed to a crawl. I turned off on a gravel entrance laid my face against the back of my hands and cried for what seemed like an eternity.

The crying was interrupted only occasionally with an angst filled scream as I purged all of the poisoned emotions from my soul.

I had never had such an intense feeling of emotion before in my life as I had just experienced. It was akin to the end of a roller coaster ride when the terror and the excitement of the steep climbs, twists and turns have finished and the car you are riding in slowly eases to a stop on the tracks.

I was exhausted. I was even more exhausted than I felt after a twelve hour day of ripping apart roofs and pounding nails. I breathed heavily, like I had just finished a marathon. I leaned back against the seat of the truck and used my forearm and the back of my hands to wipe the tears that were still clinging to my face.

Nighttime was near. The sun was slipping away and the faint twinkle of stars was beginning to show themselves overhead.

I looked out the window and saw a hand painted wooden sign that pointed in the direction of a lake. I recognized the sign immediately. It was Lake Madison. It was a lake that my father and I had visited a hundred times on weekend fishing trips.

My leg shook as I pressed the clutch inward and slipped the truck into first gear. I drove along the narrow gravel entry into a parking area at the edge of the lake and stopped.

I took two deep breaths and turned off the ignition and put the pickup in gear so it wouldn't move.

Ahead the glassy smooth lake reflected the beauty of the setting sun.

The shock of everything that had happened to me was still there but the fury that I felt wasn't. The rage was replaced with numbness that I can't describe except to say that I felt disconnected from my own body. It was almost as if I was standing on the outside looking down on someone else and analyzing what they were feeling rather than what I was feeling.

My only explanation for that is that it is some sort of hard wired human defense mechanism that each of us has inside of us but which is only exposed when we are placed under extremely stressful circumstances.

My breathing was back under control. My belief in God returned from the very brief but real doubts that I had just felt. Guilt over even feeling the anger that I had experienced gently splashed against me.

I needed more time alone before I returned home to face my father. I wasn't ready to face him yet. I didn't care if my mother raced home before me or not and told of my eavesdropping or the smashing of Pastor Jim's windshield.

I found it ironic that the truck had coasted to a stop where it had, the entrance to the lake that my father and I had visited on so many happy occasions.

The birds and the crickets were calling me from the trees. I pulled my shirt out of the front of my pants and lifted it to my face to wipe my eyes. I sat and stared across the water to the wooded banks on the other side of the lake. I was searching for an opening in the trees that I could run through so I could disappear forever.

I had never felt like this before. There were no solutions to the problem that I was drowning in. The deadly waters were rising around me squeezing the life out of my nearly limp body.

I opened the door of the truck and stepped down onto the lush green grass. I walked a short distance to the edge of the lake. There was a four feet drop from the edge of the grass to the water.

I picked up a few loose stones and skipped them along the top of the water. It was a simple act that reminded me of my father. He was the one who had taught me to skip the rocks on the surface of this very lake.

I started a long one-sided conversation with God. It's likely a conversation that God has held with millions of persons whose worlds have been turned upside down. I had a lot of questions that I wanted answers to. Questions like, why my father? There were plenty of derelicts that had shit on society at every opportunity that were deserving of an insidious disease like liver cancer. The world was littered with people like Easy's foster dad who spent his days inflicting pain on undeserving targets. Then of course there were the rapists, murderers and child molesters that as far as I was concerned forfeited their rights to life when they decided to violate their victim. Why couldn't God hand one of them a death sentence instead of my father?

As I sat with my legs dangling over the edge of the lake I waited patiently for some sign that God was listening to me. I was desperate for some sign that my plight had been noticed but the conversation yielded no answers.

Then, in some inexplicable way I was somewhat comforted, not by any feeling that my father's health was going to be miraculously restored. I was certain that wasn't going to happen but I did gain some perspective on my life and my father's situation. Feeling sorry for myself was never a part of the life lessons that my father had taught me. After all it occurred to me, who had life treated more unfairly, my father or one of the many parents whose children get a terminal diagnosis every day? What kind of justification could God possibly provide to those parents that would seem reasonable? Those children's lives were taken before they ever really started. As I conjured up a dozen situations that were less fair than my own, the sorrow that I felt for myself slowly began to dissipate.

I had always been an unusual kid that way, being so introspective at a young age. I think that I was like that because of a combination of my father sharing his perspectives on life and his believe in the hereafter. He had books on the subject that I read. Some of them spooked me and some of them comforted me. The ones that I found most interesting dealt with what people described as near death experiences. Dad had a few books on this subject and each of them gave me some hope of reuniting with family after they had passed on. If there was a life beyond the physical planet that we lived on then the only thing that would be separating my father and I would be time. Eventually I would be reunited with him, grandpa and uncle Tommy. Thinking about those books gave me a renewed since of hope that I hadn't had only a few hours earlier.

Maybe God had been listening to my desperate prayers. Maybe he had given birth to the new thoughts that were popping into my head that life extended beyond the planet that we lived on.

The sun had completely set since I had stopped at the lake and regained my composure. My blood was no longer boiling like it was when I had arrived. Hours had passed since I had parked the truck.

I stood up from the grass and brushed the leaves and dirt from the back of my pants. I reached down and picked up a loose rock off the ground. The rock was flat and thin and about the size of a silver dollar. If it bounces seven times I'll go home I told myself. I had always considered seven to be my lucky number. There was no particular rhyme or reason for seven carrying any significance as a lucky number for me but I had chosen it and now superstition was forcing me to cling to that number.

I lifted my right arm and sent the stone hurling sideways. It hit the water and jumped up and then hit the water again and again until it had bounced seven times. Then just like that sun, which had set before it, the stone cut through the water's surface and disappeared.

Chapter 17

Darkness covered the countryside as I made my way home. Out where we lived other than light that reflected off of the moon and an occasional yard light there was mostly a dense pitch black. The headlights from the truck helped guide me through the narrow and remote back roads. I was dreading the conversation that I knew had to happen but the time at the lake had been good for me. I was able to collect my thoughts and soften some of the anger that had engrossed my mind and body. Dark feelings were still just below the surface of my skin but they were less pointed and I hoped that I could express them better than I would have if I had drove straight home after confronting my mother at her church.

I took the turn off of county road 86 and onto the gravel road that would bring me home. I drove the truck slowly and calmly anticipating that my father would be outside waiting for me.

As I got closer I could see the tip of my dad's cigarette glowing on the front porch. I knew when he was inhaling because the glow would get brighter for an instant. The yard light was off and the dim light from a living room lamp was the only other sign of life in the otherwise darkened home.

I turned between the bright red reflectors that marked the approach of our driveway and cruised to a stop in front of the garage.

The thin yellow light from the living room lamp cast a silhouette of my father against the back of the porch. He was expressionless and was sitting with his feet propped up off of the ground. He was staring at me, seemingly waiting for me to get out of the truck.

I took a deep breath, stepped out of the pickup and slowly made my in front of the raised porch and up the wooden steps.

My movement was far different from what it had been when my father had surprised me by coming home early the first day of summer. On that day I had bounced down the steps with the energy of ten teenage boys. That was the beginning of a summer that was still filled with hope and excitement. Now I lifted my legs as if they were pulling one hundred pound anchors. By the time I was at the top of the porch I could feel my father's cold stare upon me.

"Where you been? It's after ten o'clock."

I wanted to answer but as prepared as I was for this moment I couldn't speak. I swallowed deeply trying to rid my throat of the lump that was firmly lodged inside of it. I walked past him without speaking a word and let the screen door slam roughly behind me.

I walked into the kitchen and laid my father's keychain on the counter. I opened the cupboard and removed a drinking glass. I turned on the faucet and ran the water over my fingertips as I waited for it to run cold. I held the glass under the faucet, filled it half way and drank it in one continuous gulp.

"You didn't answer me. Where you been?"

My father had slipped into the kitchen behind me and had startled me when he unexpectedly spoke. I turned the faucet on and filled the glass again with water. I could see my father's reflection in the kitchen window in front of me.

"I called Lee. He said you never came by the hardware store."

I spoke while facing away from him. I felt like I was frozen. The hundred pound anchors that I had carried with me up the front steps now pinned my feet to the floor.

"Your money is on the counter next to the keys." The disappointment in my voice was obvious. My voice was monotone and without emotion.

"I didn't ask about the money. I asked where you've been."

A rush of energy came over me. I felt like I needed to speak or I might explode. I turned and stood face to face with him. Dad was leaning against the kitchen doorway looking weary and worn.

"Why didn't you tell me?"

Dad took a deep breath and scratched at the top of his head with his fingers.

"It's complicated", dad replied.

"When were you gonna tell me?"

"Soon", dad said softly.

"I had a right to know! You should've told me."

"Tommy".

My dad was only able to get one word out before I interrupted him.

"I should've never found out this way", I said angrily.

"You're right Tommy", my dad said in a defeated tone.

"This whole summer was one gigantic lie. We're not going to be working together! We're not going to be hunting together! Christ, we aren't going to be doing anything together." As soon as the words left my lips I turned and threw my drinking glass into the wall, smashing it to pieces.

Silence permeated the kitchen. The gentle chirping of the locusts as they chanted in a chorus outside the kitchen window was the only noise resonating through the air.

"Tommy, take a deep breath", my father said as he tried to calm me down.

"I don't want to take a deep breath", I yelled back! "Do you know what I want? I want my family back the way a family is supposed to be. I want you to be there at my high school football games on Friday nights. I want the three of us together on Christmas morning."

Dad stepped forward from the kitchen doorway towards me.

"This isn't the way I wanted you to find out".

"Why didn't you tell me sooner", I pleaded.

"I tried", my father said in a somewhat exasperated voice. "There were a hundred times I wanted to tell you this summer but I couldn't. I didn't know how to tell you. I would sit out there on the porch or in my truck and I would plan it all out inside of my head and then, I'd see you and the joy that you had in your face and I just couldn't take that away from you, at least not right then."

"Do you think finding out on my own was supposed to be better?"

"I can't explain it Tommy. I had the words and I knew what I wanted to say. I had them right there", he said as he pointed to his mouth. "And then I would look you in the eyes and all I would see is this incredible amount of excitement and, and you'll do anything so that you won't disappoint your kids".

My father stared with glassy wet eyes. I wasn't really mad at him in particular. I was mad at the world. I was mad at God. I'm sure my father could see the anger that was bubbling inside of me. I was disappointed that my father hadn't told me that he was sick much sooner. But despite my disappointment, I never loved my father more than I did at that moment.

"Why Dad? Why did this have to happen to you?"

"I don't know kiddo", he said meekly.

I had never really been angry with my father before. I had no hatred for him and I found that even being mad at him for more than a few seconds was unnatural for me.

I took two steps forward quickly to my father's side and hugged him in a tight embrace. I nearly knocked him over as I charged into him. I couldn't hold back the tears any longer that were fighting to escape. My voice cracked as I spoke to him.

"What am I gonna do without you?"

"You're tough", he said as he squeezed my face against his chest. "When you need me, I'll always be one short prayer away".

"I just don't understand. Yesterday everything was so perfect."

"Everything just seemed perfect yesterday Tommy. Today you found the truth."

I relaxed my arms and released the grip I had on my father. We separated and stood a few feet apart from each other. I wiped at my eyes with the back of my hands. My father never wanting to spoil the image of the strong persona smiled ever so slightly turning the corners of his mouth upward.

"What are we supposed to do now?"

"Come on", dad said as he motioned with his hand.

"What about the glass I broke? I have to clean it up".

"Forget about the glass. It's not going anywhere".

Dad turned and walked back out onto the front porch and I followed closely behind him. He immediately struck a match, lit a cigarette, walked to the far end of the porch and leaned against the railing.

He coughed harshly as he smoked. He leaned over the railing with his arms resting on the top of it, spitting the phlegm as he coughed it up.

Dad's posture was hunched over. There were only twenty feet of weathered beaten planks between the two of us but to me it felt like we were standing at opposite ends of the universe.

A set of headlights broke the black cover of darkness down the road and drove in the direction of our house. Few cars traveled the road in front of our house and even fewer at this time of night. The headlights gained speed as they grew closer and then just about 100 feet before our driveway they suddenly slowed.

I recognized the outline of the car through the night air. It was my mother's sedan, she was finally returning home. Before she had a chance to park the car I made my move.

"I'm going to bed. I'm beat."

I turned and went into the house and secluded myself in my bedroom. I closed the door and lay on top of my bed softly tossing a baseball up into the air over and over again and catching it with my bare hands.

A short time later as I lay there I heard the muffled conversation of my parents. I slipped my jeans off of my legs and laid them on the floor beside the bed and curled up underneath the bed covers.

I pulled the blanket up over my chest. It was much cooler tonight than it had been on any other recent night. When the temperatures dropped like they did on this evening I usually slept better than on the hot and muggy summer nights. The day's events had exhausted me mentally and I slipped into a deep sleep.

September was approaching fast and the promises that had brought in the warmth of the summer were now fading as quickly as the days on the August calendar.

Chapter 18

Monday marked the beginning of the final week of summer. Instead of waking up with my dad shaking me by the shoulder I woke to the bright light of the September sun shining through my bedroom window.

I rolled onto my side so I could get a clear view of my clock radio. It was 10:37 a.m. five hours later than the time that I had been waking up at all summer long.

I slipped out from underneath the quilt that covered my bed and found my way into the hallway. I could see my father sitting at the kitchen table reading the newspaper. He looked up from the newspaper for just a moment as my bare feet slapped against the hard oak floors.

"Aren't we working today?" I asked in a concerned voice.

"We've worked enough this summer. I figured we'd take the day off and go up to Lake Madison and do a little fishing".

Dad turned to the next page of the newspaper and continued reading. I went to the cupboard to get a bowl for some cereal. I noticed a coffee cup with a tea bag strung over the side of it sitting on the kitchen counter. It was a telltale sign that my mother wasn't too far off.

"Where's mom?"

"In our bedroom I guess", dad answered without lifting his attention from the newspaper in front of him.

"What is she doing?"

"Why don't you go and see."

There was something unusual about my father's demeanor, especially considering everything that had unfolded last evening. He was more relaxed than I would have expected him to be.

I sat the cereal bowl on the kitchen counter and went to the pantry for a box of cereal. I took my time pouring the cereal into the bowl as I contemplated whether I wanted to face my mother again.

I could see that my father was watching me as his eyes occasionally drifted their gaze in my direction.

I poured some milk over the cereal, placed the milk carton back in the refrigerator and stirred the cereal with a spoon.

I grudgingly walked down the hallway to my parent's bedroom. The door was flung open so I stepped inside. There was a suitcase sitting on top of the bed folded open at the hinges. My mother emerged from the walk-in closet and walked toward me cradling a stack of folded clothes in her arms.

She looked at me with a blank expression normally reserved for a mannequin.

"Your father said that the two of you spoke", she said as she took the stack of folded clothes she had been cradling and set them on the bed.

"Your father and I had a long conversation last night." My mother lifted the clothes one piece at a time and carefully arranged them in the baby blue colored suitcase. "Now that there aren't any secrets we decided it would be best if I were to move. I can stay at the church for free. It's nothing fancy but I'll have a bed, a shower and a chance to make some money by helping out in the office. It will be the best for everyone."

"For everyone", I questioned sarcastically.

"You had best get a grip on that temper of yours! You're lucky you didn't hurt Pastor Jim. His throat is bruised and his car window is ruined. I'm surprised he didn't call the police."

I wanted to lash out at my mother so badly but I bit down on my tongue hard to avoid another fight.

"Vandalizing a car and then smashing a glass against the kitchen wall, that's an unhealthy way to manage your emotions wouldn't you agree?"

"What did dad have to say about you staying at the church?"

My mother had been in constant motion since I had entered the bedroom. Her nervous energy had her running in an oval but my words grabbed her attention and she finally stopped moving for a moment and stood with her arms crossed just a few feet away from where I was.

"You're father and I have been having problems for a long time. I mean, our problems started way before he ever had any idea that he was sick. Frankly for you to pass judgment on me like I'm some sort of cold hearted bitch isn't fair."

"You don't really want to preach to me about what is fair and what isn't fair right now do you?"

"Actually I do. I'm still you're mother and if I want to give you a lecture that's my business."

"Yeah and I'm old enough to make some decisions too, but I will never make the same mistakes that you have."

"Never say never Tommy because life has a way of making you eat your words, especially when you start acting so high and mighty."

My mom continued to pick the folded clothes off of the bed and place them strategically inside of the suitcase. She was trying to maximize every square inch of space within the hard shell case.

"Once Pastor Jim gets transferred to Des Moines I'll be following him there. There's no need to run off and tell your father. He's aware of everything. There's nothing you can tell him that he doesn't already know."

My mother returned to the closet speaking to me as she picked through several small boxes curious as to their contents. She stacked them up and then balanced them in her hands as she used her chin to steady the boxes at the top of the stack.

"You could have come with me but now that you attacked Pastor Jim that's out of the question and I don't blame him."

"Don't blame him for what, ruining my parent's marriage.

My mother stopped packing again. Apparently my parent's state of marriage was like an exposed nerve. It was both raw and painful to the touch.

"Our marriage has been over for a long time Tommy. We just never did anything to acknowledge that it was done. I'm sorry it ended like this but I'm not about to sit here and let a fourteen year old tell me how to live my life."

"I'm your son. Doesn't that mean anything to you?"

"I've never stopped loving you or caring about you Tommy", my mother said in a frank voice. "Right now I just need to take care of myself."

"And I need to take care of Dad. I guess it works out best for both of us."

My mother went to the dresser and pulled open two more drawers. She went about the business of packing her clothes and personal items without making eye contact with me.

"Your father has arranged for you to live with your Aunt Gloria when everything is done."

"What does that mean exactly when you say when everything is done? Is that a Christian way of saying when dad is dead?"

"We're your parents. We need to make sure you're taken care of."

I could tell that my mother's patience was wearing thin.

"You can make me out to be some unfeeling, heartless person but I know who I am on the inside and more importantly God knows."

"God may know but I don't know. Who are you anyway? You're not the same person who used to care about what happened to me at school every day."

I turned around and left my parent's bedroom. I didn't care to hear the answer to my question. I had made my feelings known to her. She was heartless as far as I was concerned. There was nothing she was going to say to me that was going to excuse the infidelity she had taken part in while my father was dying.

I walked back to the kitchen so I could sit down and eat breakfast with dad but the only thing at the kitchen table was a neatly folded newspaper.

I pulled the chair that I normally sat in back away from the table and set my bowl of cereal next to my father's empty place setting.

It gave me a strange feeling. His chair was pushed in and his breakfast dishes had been moved to the sink. The only sign that he even existed was the newspaper that had been left behind. I knew that waking to the sight of my father sitting at the kitchen table would soon be only a memory.

The future was about to look very different from the past I had experienced. Life was about to reveal a lot of changes to me that were unforeseen as recently as a few weeks ago.

My future could be described with one word, uncertainty. The only thing certain about my future was that it wouldn't resemble my life to be as I had envisioned it. Each day I would be waking to the unknown. I would be following a darkened trail without as much as a map to guide me. It was in fact no different than the road that most persons follow through life except that I now knew what many people four times my age haven't yet realized, the passageway we walk through life changes with every footstep that we take.

Chapter 19

I was sitting alone at the kitchen table eating from a bowl of cold cereal that was holding down a red and white checkerboard tablecloth when I heard the telltale sounds of my father's large boots walking up the porch steps.

The screen door squeaked open as it stretched the rusty tension spring that kept it from blowing off of its hinges. The winds could become quite vicious with very little warning in the blustery South Dakota prairie wind.

"Get dressed", my dad directed. "I already got the fishing rods and the tackle boxes in the back of the truck."

I took up what was now my familiar position in the driver's seat of dad's truck. I was now officially in charge of driving duties. My dad had turned over that responsibility to me. He seemed to enjoy sitting in the passenger seat and taking in the country scenery without having to worry about the road in front of him.

"Remember the first time I took you up there?"

"Not really."

"Oh come on. You really don't remember? You had a fishing pole about this long." My dad held his hands out in front of him no more than two feet apart from each other.

"It was a cute fishing rod. I think it was a birthday present".

Dad was sitting with his back leaned against the passenger door and his legs stretched forward in front of him at a forty five degree angle. His boots pressed against the rubber floor mat that he kept inside the truck.

A smile came over my father's face as he began to tell me the story of our first fishing trip. The memory of that first fishing pole of mine was waking happy memories that had been slumbering inside of him.

"Did we catch anything?" I asked curiously.

"Catch anything", dad said in a flabbergasted voice. "I don't think we even got our fishing hooks into the water."

I calmly turned down the same road that less than a day earlier I had driven down in a rage.

"Why not?"

"Well, first of all like most five year olds you had the attention span of a gnat. Somewhere between the butterflies that kept dancing through the air around us and the frogs the kept bending the tall grass we were sitting on you completely forgot about fishing. I ended up following you around to make sure you didn't get to close to the edge of the lake and fall in."

I turned to the right up a short bumpy road and gently parked the truck in the shade that was cast down by a pair of giant maple trees. Their leaves had changed to a beautiful golden orange color as Mother Nature began to send a subtle reminder to anyone who was paying attention that the change of seasons was upon us.

Dad opened the passenger door of the truck and leaned against it for a moment taking in a couple of long deep breaths before joining me alongside the bed of the pickup. I grabbed both fishing rods and he reached over and took the tackle boxes and the carton of bait we had brought with us.

Together we walked along the side of the lake to the edge of two giant boulders that we had adopted as our own somewhere over the years and the many days we had spent on the shoreline. I sat on the boulder to the left as we faced the lake and my father sat on the boulder to the right. They were our unofficial seats whenever we visited Lake Madison.

It was chilly for the middle of a late September afternoon yet I noticed that my father had several beads of sweat forming on his forehead.

Dad pulled a hanky from his rear pocket and dabbed away the perspiration.

"Are you okay dad?"

"Oh yeah, I'm alright. It's nothing but a little fever. I took the back of my hand and held it up my father's forehead the same way that my mother had done to me so many times when I was feeling ill.

"You're burning up dad."

"Horseshit. I'm fine. It's nothing a couple of Tylenol can't fix."

Dad reached down and picked up the carton of worms.

"So after you got bored with the frogs and the butterflies I sat you down to show you the worms like these."

Dad took the round Styrofoam carton of night crawlers and held it up while he plucked a couple of the worms out with his right hand.

"I picked up the worms just like this and you took one into your hands and watched it as it squirmed back and forth across your fingers. You loved it. You weren't afraid at all. Some kids wouldn't have touched those things but not you. In fact you liked them a little bit too much."

"Oh God, please don't tell me I ate one", I said with a look of horror.

"I took the worm from your hands and just before I stuck the hook through him you let out a scream that scared every fish that was within a hundred miles of us straight to the bottom of the lake. I mean I thought you might have gotten bit by a rattlesnake or something. You scared the piss out of me."

"You screamed because you didn't want me to stick the worm with the fishing hook. That's when I officially knew you weren't going to be the next great fisherman."

"I was a baby."

"You were not. You were five years old."

"Well I didn't want to hurt him", I said defensively.

"And we didn't. We sat like a couple of halfwits with ours fishing lines in the water and no bait on 'em. You were somehow convinced that the fish would still bite at the empty hooks."

"Were you mad?"

"No way, I remember that afternoon like it was yesterday. I've forgotten about a whole bunch of fishing trips that we've taken since then but that fishing trip, I'll never forget that one."

Dad and I looked at each other for a long time smiling and silent. He finished baiting the hooks and we cast the lines into the water. A new bead of sweat formed on my father's forehead. He reached back into his pocket for his handkerchief and brought it upward to a point just below his hairline. He wiped off the sweat again and put the handkerchief back into his pocket knowing he would be pulling it out over and over again. When his hand came back into view he had a wrinkled pack of cigarettes in its place. I hadn't noticed until now but my father hadn't smoked a single cigarette the entire time we had been driving and sitting on the rocks by the lake.

He noticed me staring as he stuck the cigarette in between his lips.

"What?"

"Nothing, I just noticed that you haven't had a cigarette yet today."

Dad seemed surprised by my observation.

"Yeah, well they don't taste too good right now."

Dad reached into his other pocket and pulled out a stainless steel lighter and with his hands cuffed he brought the cigarette to life.

The fishing trip had been a success. I hadn't thought once about the misery that I had endured the night before and it had given me a memory that I would always carry with me; the story of my first fishing trip with my father when butterflies and frogs were still magical.

Chapter 20

It was a brisk and breezy evening for early October. Dad and I were sitting on the porch in the front of the house. There was a steady stream of waves of cool air that the night sent spilling over us.

Despite the chilly fall air, it was both comfortable and peaceful on the front porch. I loved looking into the endless curtain of stars that were sprinkled over the blackened sky.

Closer to where we sat a yellow glow softly emanated from the yard light, which hung flimsily from the peak of our garage.

The only sounds out here this time of night were the steady hum of the crickets, the howling of the wind and the rattling of the leaves against one another in the trees that lined the property. Occasionally the sound of tires pressing against the gravel road that passed in front of our house would make themselves heard but traffic on our road was sparse.

Dad had fallen into a reverse pattern of sleeping during the day and waking during the evening. He preferred to be awake during the nighttime. It was cooler at night and with frequent fevers the cool night air was more comfortable.

We both savored the smell of the oak and the elm trees as they burned in our fireplace. Their sweet aroma swirled out of the top of our roof through the red brick chimney and into the shadowy autumn sky.

This was our time to talk or to sit quietly and listen to the sounds of the darkness that surrounded us.

Tonight all of the usual sounds of nighttime were joined by the occasional formation of geese that honked and squawked as they flew overhead.

"Old man winter is coming early this year", dad said as he followed the sounds of the geese through the darkened sky.

The hundreds of geese that had been making their way overhead was a surefire sign of winter weather looming in the not so distant future.

As the wind blew through the branches of the giant maple that we had planted in memory of uncle Tommy it shook some of the leaves loose and sent them twirling toward the ground.

I stared into the nothingness of the eastern sky. The moon was crescent shaped and hovered just above the horizon line.

I was wearing a heavy hooded sweatshirt. It was tattered and faded but it served as just the right barrier between my skin and the bitter fall air. Dad was dressed for the weather as well in blue jeans, a plaid flannel shirt and his signature boots. He had a quilt folded in his lap just in case the temperature grew cooler while he sat on the porch.

"It's been so quiet out here this week. Have you noticed?"

"Not really", I answered as I shook my head back and forth.

Everything seemed like every other October I had experienced. The color changes that graced the tops of the trees, the sun setting a little earlier every evening and the sight of the combines moving swiftly through the fields as they cultivated the crops and picked up the grains. These were all the usual sights of October.

"This time of year the winds usually gust at night. It's just too still out here for October."

Dad was very wise when it came to the weather. He knew the forecast better than the television weatherman did most of the time. He used a combination of his instinct and the experience he had gained from the many falls and winters that he had endured.

"This is what they call the calm before the storm. It's "old man winter" playing possum."

Dad knew that the unusually quiet week had been nothing more than a mirage. It's like that elusive wet spot that can be found on the highway as you drive. It is just out of your car's reach on the blacktop and you can chase it all day long under the torrid summer sun without out ever catching it. The sun and the tar team together to lull our brains into believing that something is sitting out there just beyond the reach of our tires when in reality it's nothing more than an illusion.

Dad was out of character this evening. He was restless and I could tell that his mind was contemplating more than the inevitable change of seasons that happens each fall. I sat on the porch quietly even though I ached to know what thoughts were racing through his mind.

When he finally began to speak his true feelings I sensed that he had rehearsed the conversation the same way a stage actor rehearses the lines of a Shakespearian play. I sensed a fear in his voice that I had never heard before. In my lifetime, I had never seen my father fear anything before that Sunday when I caught him in tears while speaking with my aunt Gloria. His fear on that day had less to do with concern about himself than it did with his concern for how I would handle his premature death.

Life up to this point had dealt my father poverty, blizzards, tornados, war and the untimely death of his kid brother. Until now though, I had only seen the concerned look which he bore on his face that one fateful afternoon.

His expression spoke volumes. Little did I know his fear this evening stemmed not so much from death's tightening grip but rather from the details of a plan that he had forged in his mind over the past several months.

My father was holding on tightly to his most private thoughts. Occasionally he would reminisce about the good times, the holidays past and the summer days that we had spent sitting along the banks of Lake Madison fishing for bullheads and catfish.

As we conversed, I sensed that my father was merely buying time so that he could build up his courage to speak to me about what really was on his mind.

I listened and smiled as he reminisced about some of our most prized moments. Each sleeping memory that he woke inside of me provided me with warmth and comfort. I knew that evenings like this were precious and that they needed to be savored and embraced as the treasures that they were.

Dad had spent hours wallowing in long stretches of silence. What does someone who is contemplating his or her mortality think about I wondered? Are they more concerned about what they are leaving behind or what lies ahead of them? The greatest mystery of all still is whether death is an ending or a beginning and that question must cross the paths of the minds of those who are most near life's end.

My dad had always been a Christian. He believed in heaven, hell, God, and the spirit world. He was curious about what was in store for him in the afterlife.

He was also focused on my well-being. I wanted to comfort him by telling him that I would be fine and that things were going to be okay but each time I was ready to bring the subject up I instead sat silently with my voice paralyzed by fear.

The truth was that my father didn't need me to remind him of his destiny? I held my tongue as we sat there side by side, enjoying the serenity of the night. The security I felt by having my father next to me was a security that would soon be lost forever. I wanted to appreciate every day, every night, and every conversation that remained.

"I've been doing a lot of thinking Tommy. I'm sure I don't have to tell you that. You see me when I'm sitting here. You can tell that my mind is restless. Sometimes when I'm lying in bed the thoughts inside my head are racing around so quickly that I can't finish thinking about one before I start thinking about another. My mind is always awake and spinning. It damn near drives me crazy sometimes."

Dad cupped his left hand over the tip of an unlit cigarette and held it to the flame of his lighter. He took two long, deep drags from the end of it and then turned his head away from me and exhaled. He was building up courage, something that I had been unable to myself for weeks now. He was finally starting the conversation that had been lodged somewhere between his brain and his vocal chords.

"I have to be honest with you. I know I can because you've got a level head on your shoulders."

Dad exhaled again and the smoke was quickly whisked away into the cool night air.

"A year ago I would have never dreamed that we would be living here alone without your mother having a conversation like this but that just goes to show you how strange and unpredictable life can be sometimes. Listen to me, I'm old enough to know how quickly lives can be turned upside down but I never thought this could happen to me until a few months ago."

I intertwined my fingers clenching them tightly into one ten fingered fist and nervously moved my right foot in a circular motion. I knew better than to speak and interrupt my father. I knew that he had probably lit a hundred cigarettes on the porch intending to have this conversation with me. Yet, each time he had built up the courage to talk to me he had stopped himself short of speaking to me like he was right now.

"It seems I spent my whole life planning for a day that I'm never gonna see. I made a lifetime of decisions; I mean we're talking huge life changing decisions planning for a fictitious day that I believed would someday be there waiting for me. I was sure that I had it all figured out but that's the irony of life, it's a journey with all kinds of turns in the road and until you make that next turn you're never really gonna know what lies around that corner."

Dad reached into his jacket, pulled out a fresh cigarette and replaced the one he had just finished smoking. He struck the lighter with his thumb again creating a yellowish golden glow for just a moment in the otherwise jet black night air. He inhaled and exhaled in a slow and deliberate rhythm, using the deep breaths to calm himself so he could continue talking to me. Then he rested the cigarette between the same two fingers that he always did on his right hand. He looked over at me gauging whether he had my full attention or not.

"There are all kinds of mistakes that a person can make during their life. The one real important thing though is that you need to make your mistakes small ones so that you can learn from them and go on without ever second guessing yourself."

Dad stopped speaking to do what he did so frequently now, to gasp for a breath of air while a deep and throaty cough rattled out of his throat.

"I've learned two things for sure; you can't change the past and you can't predict the future. If you look backward or forward too long you're gonna miss out on that day that is sitting right there in front of you."

His words moved in harmony with his right hand. His cigarette was bouncing in the air expressively as he held his right arm fully extended in front of him. He moved it with short but intense bursts of motion punctuating the sentences with the fiery end of it.

"That's kind of deep isn't it? I'm probably starting to sound like one of them Greek philosophers. The thing is Tommy, life is so complicated. That's why the brightest scientists in the world still only understand a fraction of how our brains function. The most complex computers in the world are still mounted inside of our skulls."

I forced a smile telegraphing to him that I understood while still being careful not to interrupt him.

"You see I always tried to play it safe." Dad stopped speaking and looked at me with a quizzical look on his face. "Do you know what I mean? I tried to control everything and because of that I made some decisions that I wish I wouldn't have made."

Dad knew that he had my attention. Our eyes were connected by an invisible laser like rope that hung tightly in the air connecting us.

"Like the decision I made to stop working on grandpa's farm. I loved farming but I gave it up so I could make a life for myself that was more secure. I wanted a job where I didn't care how much rain fell in the summer or how quickly the springtime thaw came. I passed up family vacations so I could do what, save a few dollars? Those are the decisions that I regret. If I could take that money that I have in my savings account and trade it in for one more summer vacation with you I would do it in the blink of an eye. I want you to know that. I thought I was making the right decisions at the time. My intentions were good. I was trying to build a future for you but now I won't be there with you to share it anyway. I guess it just wasn't part of God's plan for us. I worked a lot of long hours to save money so that your mom and I would have a safety net. It would be a little money to help us out if we got in a financial jam. Now look at what I sacrificed and look at what I got in return. For all of those long hours and all of those late nights that I wasn't there for you I've got a few bucks in the bank. Those dollars can't buy me my health back so what difference did it make that I saved them? The little league games I missed and the Saturdays that you were left alone here at the house while I hustled a job, those are all choices I made that I regret."

My dad took a break from speaking to me and sipped from his cup of coffee before knocking off the ash that was growing from the end of his cigarette.

Meanwhile I sat there terrified on the inside. I didn't allow my inner feelings to show themselves. On the outside, I appeared tough and unflappable just like my father always did. I wanted desperately for him to see that same quality in me. I was mature enough to know that this wasn't a conversation that any father ever wanted to have with his teenage son. I wasn't about to make it any more difficult for him. He had been strong for me on so many occasions and now I had to be strong for him. I needed him to believe that I would be able to fend for myself and carry on in my life despite the tragedy of our circumstances.

I knew this was one of those moments that I would look back on when dad wasn't here to speak with and when I was in need of advice. He was trying to prepare me for those times when I would be alone. I felt it had to be torturing him to know that he wouldn't be there for me ten years from now when I might be starting my own family.

As the cigarette he was holding burned nearly to the end of his fingertips, he pulled a fresh cigarette from the pack he kept in his pocket and snuffed out the spent cigarette on the porch with the heel of his boot.

In spite of a cough that had progressively worsened all summer long there was no indication that my father was ever going to stop smoking. Dad puffed and exhaled with deep relaxing breaths in between sporadic and spastic coughing spells. He sipped from his coffee cup moistening his lips and allowing the cool coffee to spill down his throat to lubricate and soothe it.

"I've been thinking for a while now Tommy. You might only be fourteen years old on paper but you're closer to being a man than you are to being a child. You can stand on your own two feet. I saw that all summer. You grew up a lot these past few months. Even though you're going to be living with Aunt Gloria, I know you could make it on your own if you had to."

I remained nervous and afraid on the inside but I continued to hide my true emotions. I listened intently never allowing my attention to drift.

"I was a lot older than you when my dad passed away and I know how hard that was for me. I knew the end for him was coming for almost a year. I had these bizarre thoughts enter my head at the strangest times. They would take over my mind. I could be sitting in the truck at a red light with the radio crackling and sheets of raindrops pounding the windshield but I wouldn't notice the rain and I wouldn't hear the crackle of the radio. It was like, life was happening all around me but my own little universe never extended beyond the thoughts that were circulating through my head."

I straightened my shoulders and pushed myself up in my chair never looking away from my dad's piercing blue eyes.

"I realized that I didn't see the rain because I was thinking about something that I wished I would have asked my father when I still had the chance. I didn't hear the radio because I thought of all of the time that he spent alone in his bed while he was sick and I wasn't there to comfort him."

Dad moved his tongue around the outside of his lips. He was badly dehydrated.

"I'm not going to be there to give you advice when you face the tough questions that we all have to face in life. I'm telling you right now that whatever you do, listen to your heart. You'll always make the right decision if you listen to your heart."

I could feel the lining of my throat tightening. It was becoming harder and harder for me to hide my feelings. I was in no condition to speak so I nodded my head back and forth and swallowed deeply.

"It's going to be hard sometimes Tommy, I'm not going to lie to you. It's going to be really hard but I'll be watching and I'll be listening. You'll always know that I'm there watching over you."

Despite the tense feeling in my throat, which was nearly choking me, I had to speak. It was too important of a moment for me not to speak.

"I sometimes wonder why this happened but who in the hell am I to question God's motives? I've had a lot of great things happen to me in my life but nothing was better than the day when you came into my life. That was a magical moment when I saw you for the first time. They handed you to me in this little white towel and there you were this tiny, wrinkled little runt of a thing not much bigger than my hand. You were so helpless and vulnerable. That's when I realized the real purpose of my life was to protect you.

I was put here to make sure that you were always safe. You're old enough now that you can do that yourself. I just thank God that I was given a chance to be there for you until you were old enough to stand on your own two feet. Someday when you're married and you have your own kids you'll know how I felt that day that you were born."

"Dad", I said trying to break into the conversation.

"Tommy, don't say it won't happen", he interrupted. "I'm telling you right now that some girl is going to walk by you in the supermarket, turn her head and look at you with her big brown eyes and trust me that's all it will take."

The wind was picking up and my father spread the quilt that rested in his lap out across his legs.

A pair of headlights came into view as a car turned off of County Road 86 and traveled on the gravel road that passed in front of our house. I hoped it wasn't my mom driving back to our house with hopes of inserting herself back into our lives. It was the first car to head in our direction since we sat down this evening. There was very little traffic where we lived. I recognized the vehicle as it drew closer. It was our neighbor, T-bird's Ford van.

T-bird was our closest neighbor in terms of proximity. His home was less than a quarter mile from our own. Even though T-bird lived a short distance away we rarely saw him. He was a recluse and his property served him well to keep him hidden away from the rest of society. His yard was lined with trees and shrubs that worked as camouflage wall to conceal his home from the rest of the world.

T-bird didn't go out of his way to be neighborly either. He had declined more than one dinner invitation from my parents. The few times I saw him in town he tipped his head forward and quickly moved past me without making any sort of acknowledgment. There was little small talk or friendly conversation with T-bird. He was content being a loner and made it known to those around him that he preferred it that way.

"I'd like to know where he is always driving to all the time. I can't imagine that he has any friends."

"Do you want some more coffee dad?"

"No. I still got some here."

Dad breathed deeply and I repositioned myself in my chair.

"Tommy when we named you after my brother it was because he was the bravest person I ever knew. We wanted to name you after someone who represented strength and courage."

Dad took out his hanky and coughed into it heartily.

"Nothing ever scared your uncle, Tommy."

"You're brave dad. I've never seen you afraid either."

"Yeah, you may not have seen it but I've been afraid. Something about your uncle was different. He didn't just seem invincible, he was invincible! You could feel it when you talked to him. He had this conviction in his voice when he spoke. It was this pure and unshakable determination. He was so passionate. I really admired that sense of adventure that lived inside of him. That and his courage, those are the main reasons why we named you after him. I was hoping some of that "thing", whatever it was that Tommy had, would rub off on you. The way he climbed into the seat of that crop duster and flew it around, it was as if he was playing with a paper airplane. He was absolutely fearless. There's no other way to describe it."

Dad looked up toward the sky for a moment, perhaps remembering the sight of Tommy's crop duster as it glided gracefully over the top of a field.

"He told me once that he felt more alive when he was soaring through the air in that little plane than he did at any other time. I've thought about that a lot lately, how the fear of death never influenced him."

As dad finished the sentence he took a long drink from his coffee cup. His mouth was dry from a combination of dehydration and the cool dry air.

"And then there was your grandfather. Grandpa was a tough son of a bitch but he was different from your uncle. Your grandfather was at the mercy of death long before it whisked him away. It seemed like all he did that last year he was around was go on doctor appointments and lay in that bed waiting for that moment when he would draw his last breath. Death didn't just take his life, it stole his identity. His nickname was moose ya know. That's what everybody called him. He didn't like much of a moose when he passed away. He had those big and broad shoulders but they ended up being nothing but skin and bones."

Dad was caught off guard by a coughing spell. He bent over at the waist as he sat and the mucus rattled inside of his chest.

"Grandpa couldn't help that he got sick just like you can't help that you got sick."

I didn't want to interrupt my father but I was confused. I knew Grandpa had suffered from cancer. He was a victim of the same disease which had now invaded my father's body. But my grandfather never chose to be sick and I'm certain he never relished the suffering that he endured as his body wasted away.

"Grandpa let the cancer kill him one day at a time until he had to be fed through a tube. Cancer took away his dignity. I won't let cancer do that to me Tommy. I want you to remember me as big and strong not with a bunch of tubes and shit coming out of me."

"I'll take care of you dad. I don't care what I have to do."

"Tommy, I'm not going to let you sit by while I wither away to some helpless pile of flesh. If it was my dog we were talking about and that dog couldn't eat or go to the bathroom anymore on his own I'd be kind enough to end his suffering with one well-placed bullet. As far as I'm concerned people should have the right to be treated with the same kindness and mercy as animals are."

Dad took a moment from speaking to observe my response to what he was saying. He took a long deep drag from his cigarette and blew a cloud of white smoke that swirled through the cool autumn air and faded into the night.

"When the time comes Tommy when I can't be myself anymore then I want you to show me that same kind of mercy."

Dad turned and stared at me. I was naïve after all. I was barely fourteen and dad had taken this conversation in a direction that I never would have imagined.

"How am I supposed to do that?"

"I'm gonna need your help. I want you to bring me back to the place where my life began, back to the family farm."

I was surprised by dad's request. I couldn't understand why he had been afraid to ask me to bring him back to the farm. I could drive now. I knew the way there from all of the times that we had made the trip together.

"We can go there whenever you want to dad. I'll drive."

I knew how much dad missed the farm at times. He spoke so fondly of his childhood memories and of the world that he had grown up in.

Dad shifted himself in his chair and moved to the edge of it so he was closer to me.

"Let me try this again Tommy."

Dad puffed on his cigarette. His eyes rolled upward in their sockets as if he were looking backward into his mind trying to find the words to explain what he was trying to say.

"It's not just that I need your help getting me to the farm Tommy. There's more to it than that."

Dad had done everything for me. I was willing to do whatever I could to help him.

"Whatever you want dad, I'll do it."

Dad interrupted me before I could finish my sentence.

"Hear me out Tommy. First of all this is between you and me. This is no one else's business. You can't talk about this with anyone."

Dad had a very serious look on his face. A look accompanied by an equally serious unblinking stare.

"You have to promise that this conversation never goes beyond this porch."

Dad waited patiently for me to affirm that promise with him before he would discuss the matter any further with me.

"I promise", I said as confidently as I could. "I won't tell anybody."

This wasn't any ordinary discussion that occurs between a father and a son. This was a man to man conversation. My father's face was wearing a look of desperation. Our relationship had grown into something more than father and son. He was treating me as his equal.

"I'm not going to waste away in some hospital bed suffering while I'm being cared for by a staff of underpaid strangers. That's not the way I'm going out of this world Tommy. This is my life and this is my choice!"

Dad was speaking with a tone of assuredness.

"It's not the government's decision or some third generation doctor from an Ivy League school who ended up working out here in the middle of nowhere because he spent more time at the local tavern as a medical intern than he did doing his homework. I'll spend every day I have left together with you as long as I'm still able to take care of myself. Do you understand?"

I nodded my head indicating that I understood but the truth is I still wasn't sure what my dad was asking of me.

"When the time comes and I'm not the man you know me to be, then I want you to bring me back to my favorite spot on the hilltop behind the house at the farm. That's where I want to die."

"But how will you know when it's your time dad?"

"I'll know."

The thought of dropping off my dad in a field and leaving him to die alone was beyond my comprehension.

"You want me to bring you up to the farm and leave you alone to die? You could freeze to death."

"No Tommy, that's not what I'm asking. I don't want to suffer. I don't want you to be wondering whether or not I'm alive or dead. I just want the quick release of my soul when the time has come."

My father must have seen the confusion swirling within my head.

"You're a great marksman now Tommy. There's a reason I've been taking you to shoot the clay pigeons all summer long. You can hit a twirling clay disc the size of a hockey puck a hundred feet away with the sun shining in your eyes. I know you can hit a spot the size of my fist from fifteen feet away when it's perfectly still."

My father reached into his jacket to an inside pocket and pulled out a stained envelope that was folded in half. and handed it to me. I held it in my hands and examined it. This was a letter that had been sitting for a while. It smelled musty, like something that has been stowed away in an attic trunk.

"That's for you", he said calmly. "I got that years ago, after uncle Tommy's crash."

I slowly unfolded the envelope and read the name of the company typed on it.

"First American Life and Casualty", I read out loud waiting for my father to fill in the blanks.

"That's an accidental death policy. It hardly pays anything if cancer rots me to death from the inside out. The thing is though, if I were to die in an accident, then it pays twenty five thousand dollars. That's enough money for you to pay your way through college."

"An accident", I questioned. I was confused. I was certain that my father was going to die from the cancer that was spreading inside of his body.

"Any accident, it doesn't matter. It can happen in a car or it can happen in a corn field. Think about it Tommy. I don't want to suffer like grandpa did. I'm dying anyway. Why make me suffer through a few weeks of misery when I can go out on my terms and you can have the chance to go to college."

"Dad, how do you expect me to shoot you? I love you."

"You're looking at this the wrong way Tommy."

His tone intensified as he went down to one knee in front of me as I sat on the porch. He was at my level. Our faces were only inches apart from each other. His eyes were alive and almost bursting from their sockets. His neck was tight causing all of blood vessels and tendons to protrude.

"Because you love me is why you can do it. You don't want the people that you love to suffer."

I was quiet, maybe out of shock from my dad's request.

"What about prison", I questioned.

"Tommy, do you remember that doe that we found on the side of the road. She was alive wasn't she? She didn't have any hope of leaving that place. She was gonna die it was just a matter of time. I brought her peace. I stopped her pain. I did the right thing!"

My father became more demonstrative as he spit out each sentence.

Nothing that my father could have asked of me would have surprised me more than his request on this night. It was obvious to me he had given this a lot of thought. He was eerily calm about the request. None of what he was asking of me seemed to be extraordinary to him. I had a good idea now what my dad had been contemplating each night as he sat on the porch this summer.

"Tommy, listen to me. We can make it look like an accident. It's your first hunting trip with a new gun, your feet get tangled in a clump of dirt, you trip, your finger hits the trigger and your gun goes off. End of story."

"Dad, I don't know. I'm afraid."

My father was determined to sell me on his deadly plan.

"Tommy, you tell me what's more humane, dying instantly from a gunshot or wasting away for weeks in a strange bed while you're being taken care of by a bunch of people you don't know?"

And just like that, the conversation I had that night with my father would change my life forever. My life would be changed in the same way that my aunt's life had been changed when my uncle Tommy crashed his plane.

I knew my dad would never force me to carry out his dying wish. He wanted to make sure that it was something I could live with as well. He turned his head away from me. Dad tipped his head downward. A discouraged look streamed from his eyes into the darkness of the dimly lit porch.

"I don't know dad. I need time to think."

Dad turned his head back up. He reeked of desperation. His eyes were teary and his tone was determined.

"One way or the other I'm going out on my terms. If you can't help me end the pain then I understand, but I'm still going to need a ride up there."

Dad stood up and walked to the storm door. As he walked by me he gently patted me on the shoulder. It was a gesture to let me know that he respected whatever decision I arrived at.

I stayed out on the porch numbed not from the cold air but from the circumstances that I found myself in. I stared out into the nothingness of the dark countryside. I watched the branches on the maple tree as the gusts of wind caught the leaves that remained and bent the branches downward. Maybe I could plant a tree in memory of dad. It would be a living memory in the same way that my father had planted a tree in memory of Uncle Tommy. I would put it alongside the driveway next to the maple planted in uncle Tommy's memory. The two trees could be companions on the hillside. After all, the silence of the desolate area that we lived in could be comforting but it could also be chilling. A scream out here evaporates into the thin cool air long before it reaches the ears of a neighbor. It's a remote area where a fallen body could decay for months or years without being noticed.

At the moment I was feeling more of the isolation of the country than the peacefulness that it could bring.

The feeling of isolation was only amplified by being faced with a decision that I couldn't speak to anybody about.

I wrestled internally with the thought of shooting my father. I understood that it was more humane to spare someone a natural death with a disease that could inflict the kind of misery like cancer was known to cause. I didn't know if I could shoot my own father even when the reason was to spare him physical pain.

I spent a long time sitting alone on the porch contemplating the idea when I finally felt that my eyes had grown weary enough that I could sleep.

Inside on top of my bed I spent the rest of the evening taking turns between lying on my right side and my left side and never really sleeping.

I stared at the ceiling, the door, and the wall at the foot of my bed. I caught a glimpse of my birthday gift resting so innocently in my gun rack. I got out of bed, walked to the wall where it was hanging and removed it from the felt lined holders that it sat in. In my hands I held the tool that could provide an instant release of my father's soul if I allowed it to. I looked at the nightstand beside my bed. On top of my nightstand were the two unspent shotgun shells that I had been twirling between my fingers on the night of my birthday. I could do it I thought. I didn't need to wait until we drove back to the family farm. He was suffering right now. I could end the pain tonight and release his soul to the heavens.

I walked back to my bed and laid the shotgun on the quilt. I felt like I was floating more than walking as I moved the gun to my bed.

I loaded the two shotgun shells into the gun and pumped it once moving a shell into the chamber ready to be fired.

As I opened the bedroom door the wooden floor felt exceptionally cold on my feet. There was a noticeable chill in the air. A breeze was blowing directly into my face as I walked like a zombie down the hallway and into my parent's bedroom. Dad was snoring loudly. One well placed shot would end his suffering in an instant. I could see where his chest was rising and falling as he was breathing. I decided that would be my target area. A head shot would leave a horrific wound and disfigure him. A chest shot would cause a mortal wound but it wouldn't compromise my father's physical appearance at his funeral.

I can do this I said to myself confidently.

I raised the gun to my shoulder and steadied my aim. My dad woke up and watched me silently. He rose to his knees and held his arms to his sides. The position he placed himself in was similar to the way Jesus looked as he was nailed to the cross.

"Come on Tommy. You can do it", dad said as he smiled widely.

The shotgun exploded with a thunderous boom, a sound so loud that I instantly sat up in my bed shivering, sweating and realizing that I had slipped into a dream.

I looked around my bedroom. Everything was in its place. I scrambled wildly feeling in the dark on my nightstand for the two shotgun shells. My hand rand across them and I picked them up, held them to the light that beamed in through my window. The shotgun casings were intact. I looked to the wall at the end of my bed. My shotgun was in the same place it always was, hanging freely from the gun rack my father had made me.

I wiped the sweat away from my face with my bed sheet. It had only been a dream but it was more real than any that I could ever remember having.

I got myself out of bed and quietly walked down the hallway to make sure that my father was okay. I stepped on the floor and felt the coldness of it, the same feeling I had sensed in the dream when I was walking across the floor. The window was open in the bathroom and the light was on. The curtains were blowing inward from the strong breeze that was swirling outside. A rush of air followed the path of the hallway and washed over my feet like the small tide of an ocean wave.

My father's bedroom door was open. He was lying on his side. He was awake and was looking at me as I stood in the doorway to his bedroom.

"Tommy what are you doing?"

"I had a bad dream. I wanted to make sure you were okay and then I saw that the light was on in the bathroom and the window was open."

"I was pretty warm so I opened it up. I wanted to get some fresh air in here. I'm better now so you can close it if you'd like", he said wearily.

I went back to my room and tried to fall back to sleep but I had a hard time doing it. I was afraid to relive the dream again. I was afraid I might sleepwalk and play the dream out in our house.

I lay there, contemplating my future and wondering whether I really could fulfill my father's dying wish. I didn't want to disappoint him but just like he had told me to do I was trying to listen to my heart. It would be the first of many sleepless nights spent contemplating his request. I was going to need more time to make my decision.

Chapter 21

My father and I spent a lot of time on the porch of our house that October in 1983. Even though the change of seasons was upon us and the air was unusually cold we were comfortable in the outdoor setting. Dad was running a temperature most of the time and he liked the fresh cool air that was offered to us on the porch.

The giant maple that had been planted in memory of my uncle had transformed itself into a brilliant orange and red canopy of leaves. The leaves were being shed daily. They were gently coaxed by the wind to let go of the branches they were clinging to so that the country breeze could bring them to rest on the ground below.

The geese continued to fly overhead during the day but there were less and less of them each day. When the geese weren't making noise the other sounds of nature took to the forefront. The howl of a lonesome coyote could sometimes be heard over the hum of the locusts and the crickets as nighttime fell.

I left the house rarely. Usually only to get the groceries we needed or to get the mail.

My father's appetite had diminished considerably and his appearance reflected his loss of appetite. The weight loss was especially noticeable in his face, neck and around his collarbones.

Dad's weight loss brought a wave of unsettling feelings over me. I knew that with each passing day that my time with my father was nearing its end.

I returned home from the store.

"I'm back", I yelled as I came through the front door holding two sacks of groceries.

Dad came from his bedroom wearing a familiar pair of blue pajamas that he spent a lot of his time in.

"Were you sleeping?"

"I nodded out for a little bit. Did you get 'em?"

I reached into the top of one grocery sack and pulled out a carton of Pall Mall cigarettes.

"I just bought you one carton."

He opened the end of the carton and took two packs of cigarettes out. He slipped one pack into the front pocket of his pajama top. He tore open the end of the other pack of cigarettes and shook a cigarette out and placed it into his mouth. The smoking ban that my mother had enforced in our house when she lived here had been abolished by my father. He smoked cigarettes inside of our house routinely now that she was gone.

"Did you get the mail?"

"Yeah it's on the counter next to your truck keys."

Dad walked over to the counter and flipped through the mail with little interest until he came across a letter.

He looked at the return address, squinting to make out the name in the top corner.

"It's from Easy", he said excitedly.

Dad pulled a butter knife out of a kitchen drawer and carefully cut along the top of the envelope.

"These damn eyes. Can you give it a read for me?"

I took the letter from my dad and sat down with him at the kitchen table.

"Dear Bob. I have been meaning to write to you. I moved out west to Rapid City and found a job as a cement finisher. I wanted to make sure you knew how much you helped me this past year. For the first time in my life someone finally gave me a sense of belonging. I have never had that feeling before. My whole life I felt like an outsider until you came along. You have taught me a lot both about the jobs we did but also about myself. I believe everyone is put on this Earth with a purpose. You will leave this Earth having made me a better person. God bless you. Easy."

"I knew he was a good kid. He just needed someone to believe in him", dad said with a satisfied look on his face.

I handed the letter back to my father and he put it back in the envelope it had come in. The letter was good medicine for my father. I could tell the letter had my dad preoccupied. He was lost inside of his thoughts.

Dad took his coat off of the back of a kitchen chair and walked out onto the porch. His coat was wrapped around his shoulders without his arms inside of the sleeves.

I put the rest of the groceries away and then joined him out on the porch. He was standing at the rail, quietly scanning the horizon.

I sat down on a chair and tipped it on its back legs leaning my back against the wall behind me.

"Did you see any geese today when you were driving?"

"No. Actually I haven't seen any for a couple of days now."

"That's because they've already moved on. They know what lies ahead. Animals are amazing creatures. We can learn a lot from watching them. They're instincts are so much sharper than ours."

Dad left the rail and sat down on the chair next to me and lit a cigarette.

"The storms are coming early this year. That's why the birds already left to fly south."

Dad entered into a coughing spell. They had become even more violent than they were before. He reached into his pocket and grabbed a handkerchief. He held it over his mouth as he fought to catch his breath. When he pulled the handkerchief away it was splattered with blood. He held it up so I could see as the coughing spell finally reached its end.

"It's time Tommy. I can hardly eat, I'm coughing up blood and I'm growing more tired by the day."

Dad turned and faced me. I knew that this day was coming but it arrived so quickly.

"We got to go Tommy. If I wait any longer I might not get out of here. I'll be okay to wait until Saturday so plan on leaving then."

I sat quietly not knowing what to say. I wasn't in denial but I had hoped that this day wouldn't have arrived so quickly.

A long and awkward silence followed. I looked downward with my head hung. My dad seemed so focused for the event. It was an unusual demeanor for someone making plans for their final day of life. Our levels of comfort with the situation were at opposite ends of the spectrum. My father may have just been putting on a brave face for me but it seemed that he was at peace with his decision.

He reached up with his hand and messed the top of my hair.

"Kiddo, I told you I would know when it was time. It's time."

Dad stood up and made his way back into the house. I stayed out on the porch. It was a clear night and the stars were brilliant. An occasional burst of cold air would hit me from the side and send a shiver through my body. When I felt myself starting to nod off I would retreat to my bedroom and curl up underneath of my quilt. I tried to stay awake until I was in an extreme state of exhaustion, that way I would hopefully have less time to lay in bed and think about my situation.

I moved to the wooden rocking chair that dad had brought out onto the porch and pulled the blanket that he kept on the back of it over my legs. I soothed my mind one rocking motion at a time. It would be a difficult night for me to sleep now that I knew we were leaving for the farm on Saturday.

The rocking chair did work well to relax me. There was something therapeutic about the slow back and forth motion. Freud would probably say it was due to a return to our infantile stage of life and that may well be true. I burrowed more deeply under the blanket as the wind grew stronger. I noticed that occasional clouds were making their way across the sky and blocking the backdrop of the stars.

The leaves from the maple tree began to come off by the dozen. They looked like giant red and orange snowflakes as they spiraled toward the grass. The rate at which they were falling was mesmerizing. The yard light cast just enough light for me to have a good view of the maple tree. I noticed a figure moving from behind the tree and growing larger. He stopped at the base of the tree and began gathering up the leaves and placed them into a bag.

"Dad", I yelled from the porch.

The wind continued to gust and I'm not sure that he could hear me from where I stood.

I walked down the steps of the porch and headed in the direction of the maple.

"Dad! It's too cold out here for you. You need to go inside."

My words were lost in the sounds of the night. The howling of the wind made it difficult for my voice to reach to that part of the yard.

As I drew closer the man stopped picking up the leaves as clusters of them continued to fall. He leaned against the tree gazing in my direction.

"Dad, you need to go inside. It's too cold out here for you."

I was about fifteen feet away from the tree when I stopped. It wasn't my dad standing there but I recognized the face.

"It's me. Uncle Tommy."

"Uncle Tommy", I echoed in disbelief. "It can't be you. You're dead".

"I came to pick up the leaves and to get your father."

"Dad's leaving on Saturday. I'm taking him."

Uncle Tommy started picking up the leaves again. He bent at the waist and picked them up by the handful and placed them into the bag.

"Saturday is too late", he said as he gathered up the leaves. "I'm supposed to take him with me tonight".

"But I'm taking him to the farm Saturday. That was his plan."

Uncle Tommy stopped gathering up the leaves and walked past me in the direction of our house. He pushed past me shoving me aside as he hurriedly walked toward the house.

"Wait", I yelled as I chased after him.

My command was ignored as Uncle Tommy walked at a quicker pace.

"It's time Tommy. You heard your father."

"But I'm not ready. We're not leaving until Saturday."

I reached for Uncle Tommy's shoulder to stop him but he slapped my arm away.

"I'm not ready", I yelled!

Uncle Tommy walked up the steps of the porch and then stopped and faced me. His demeanor scared me and I backed away from the porch. Uncle Tommy was standing and facing me. He cackled in a devilish laughter that grew with intensity as my level of fear rose.

"I said it's time!"

The storm door opened and slammed shut and I sat up in the rocking chair confused about where I was. I breathed heavily and my heart raced. It was just another dream that was tormenting me in my sleep. As I exhaled my breath turned to a foggy mist. It was even colder now than when I had been awake before I drifted into sleep.

I wasn't sure if the dream was a product of my fears or a warning sent from beyond. I quickly went inside the house and jogged down the hall to my father's bedroom. This time he was sleeping. He was snoring loudly as his breathing sounded congested.

I went back to my bedroom afraid to fall asleep. I turned from side to side in a restless state until I saw sunlight breaking over the horizon through my window.

I was realizing my fears in my sleep and during my waking hours. There was no escape from the circumstances that I found myself in. Saturday was only two days away, two days that seemed like an eternity from now.

Chapter 22

Friday, November 4th, 1983 is a day I will never forget. The time had arrived. It had been a long day and I knew that I would have trouble sleeping as I had not slept through the night for at least two weeks. On the nights when I did fall asleep I found myself as the centerpiece to dreams that were so realistic and elaborate that when I woke from them I felt anything but rested.

It was about 11pm on Friday, earlier than normal for me to be turning in for the night but we had a long day ahead of us tomorrow. My father had hardly left his bed the past few days since he proclaimed that Saturday November 5th was going to be the day for our trip back to the farm.

I found myself going by his room every couple of hours to check on him. This evening was no different from the others with regards to my concern.

I got out of bed and walked down the hallway stopping at the doorway to his room. His door was pushed open and I could see that he was sleeping. I wanted badly to try to wake him. This would be the last night that we would ever be able to have a conversation. I walked into his room, sat on the side of his bed and gently rubbed my hand on his shoulder.

I knew that he had accepted death with more grace and dignity than most people could ever dream of doing. He had made peace with his God.

I lay down in bed next to him and wrapped my arm around him, hugging him like a child. If I wasn't going to be able to sleep I was going to spend the night comforting my father. As I lay in bed next to him exhaustion from a lack of sleep over the past several nights finally gave way and I drifted off into a deep sleep. I'm not sure how long I dozed for but when I woke snowflakes were falling by the thousands and they weren't just falling, they were racing each other to the ground.

For a moment I wondered if this was the beginning of another elaborate dream that I was having. I had been fooled twice in the past week by dreams that were so real they left me in a cold sweat when I finally awoke from them.

I blinked my eyes closed for a moment to clear my head and to refocus my vision. When I opened my eyes and looked again they were still there. Rushing past the yard light at a fierce rate and a forty-five degree angle were snowflakes. Not just a few snowflakes either but thousands of snowflakes, each of them falling in symphony with one another. I hurried to the front door of the house in my bare feet. The ground was freezing cold as I stepped onto the porch. At least four inches of snow had fallen already and there was no indication that it was going to stop snowing any time soon. Snow covered the ground and the swirling wind had it drifting into unequal piles.

I went back inside of the house and into the living room and turned on the television. Teletype ran across the bottom of the screen, Severe Winter Advisory for the following towns; Sioux Falls, Parker, Beresford, Hartford and Lake Mills.

I knew that there was no way for us to travel with the weather conditions the way they were. My father's rear wheel drive pickup could easily get stuck in a few inches of snow. Out in the country the roads were said to have snowdrifts as high as two to four feet deep.

"What's going on?"

The words startled me and I turned to find my father standing behind me.

"Take a look outside."

I stepped to the side and allowed my dad to take a look out at the snowstorm front and center.

"We won't be going anywhere right now. My truck can't get through that snow, not even with the chains on the tires. We're going to have to wait until they clear the roads."

I stood behind my father as he watched the snow fall in futility.

"Pray it stops soon Tommy. It's time."

Chapter 23

The intensity of the snowstorm slowly let up throughout the day.
It was freezing outside when dad decided that the snowstorm had waned enough to allow us to start our trip. I shoveled a path through the snow from the front porch to the pickup so that he would have an easy walk to the truck. I brushed the snow off of the truck and scraped the ice that had built up on the windshield.
It was a quiet ride in terms of conversation but the inside of my head was not quiet; it was full of questions and doubts.
I had the rear view mirror positioned so I could watch dad as he sat in the passenger seat. His eyes were closed and he had a pillow wedged between his head and the doorframe. A patchwork quilt was wrapped snuggly around his legs and feet. There was a stiff wind outside making the already cold air temperature even colder.
Was he sleeping? Was he praying? Was he having a quiet internal reflection of his life? I wanted badly to ask him but my voice was as frozen as the rain that had showered over the pine and maple trees the night before.
The storm had left a beautiful backdrop on the world outside of that pickup cab. The leafless branches of the trees were coated with a shiny layer of ice. The

maples resembled giant wooden ice sculptures. The pine tree branches sank under the weight of the wet snow and ice and hung low. The sun sat high in the sky, so high in fact that it sent little in the form of warmth to us down below.

I turned to my right to get a look at dad. He was still quietly leaning against the passenger door. I drove slowly and cautiously. The conditions for driving were less than perfect. I wanted to make the ride as peaceful and smooth as possible for him. I had put several sandbags in the bed of the pickup. We did that every winter to add weight over the wheels and give a little extra traction to the giant knobby tires.

Traffic was light and the road was lonely. There were only a few towns between our house and the farm but there were miles of road to cover. The questions raged on inside of my head as I drove taking in the beauty of the early snowstorm and the ugliness of reality three feet to my right.

There was no turning back; I had promised my father that I would bring him back to the family farm and I was going to fulfill my dying fathers wish. I owed it to him. He had suffered long enough. Wanting him to suffer any longer would have merely been selfish on my part. My mind replayed that moment when he had the tearful conversation with my Aunt Gloria. He had cried only because he felt like he was letting me down in some way. Nobody chooses to be stricken with cancer. I knew he was afraid of leaving his only son without the guidance that a father can provide. I was not about to let him down.

After all, children are left parentless every day. There is always a war raging somewhere in the world. Children lose their parents without any forewarning. At least I had time to prepare for this moment. A chance to say goodbye and tell him I loved him. I was grateful for that.

Many children are not ever provided with that opportunity. They find out in the middle of the night through a phone call or a knock on the door.

It was my turn to be strong. It was my turn to comfort him.

I looked at dad as he slouched against the door. He had only had water for the past two days. His lips were chapped and puckered. His skin had yellowed and his once thick black mass of hair was now patchy. Even his hair had been robbed of the luster that life had once given it. Death, which had started at the inner core of his body, had now extended itself to the tips of his hair.

As I turned my head back to the road ahead of me, two deer stood motionless and statuesque in the middle of the road. There was not enough room to swerve around them and I instinctively jammed my foot down on the brake pedal. The truck slid left and then right, narrowly missing the deer as they leaped from the road and into the ditch. The truck came to rest sideways in a snow bank that had been left behind by the snowplows when they had cleared the road.

My dad sat up, opened his eyes and calmly said, "Be careful. There are a lot of deer around here."

The deer were attracted to the salt left behind by the snowplows on the icy road. Two hundred yards away in the soft blanket of snow that covered the pasture the deer stood unharmed and staring in our direction.

"How did you know there were deer on the road? I was looking at you. Your eyes were closed."

"Tommy, how could I see the deer if my eyes were closed."

The corners of his mouth crinkled forming a miniature smile. He looked different from the man I was looking at just minutes earlier. Even his eyes looked less cloudy and his skin didn't seem to have the same yellowish tint that it had held moments before. His smile widened and he gave me his patented wink. He sat upright adjusting the quilt so it was not wrapped so tightly around his legs.

"Tommy, put it in reverse. Get us back on the road."

I faced forward and turned the ignition. The truck started without any hesitation. Something strange was happening but I didn't know what it was.

I looked in the rearview mirror and in a whispered tone my dad was speaking. So softly he spoke that I couldn't hear him, but I watched as he smiled and his lips continued to move stopping occasionally as if he was pausing to listen. I backed the truck away from the snow bank, slipped it into first gear and made my way back onto the highway. Finally, I turned my head to the right.

"Dad, I can't hear you."

His lips stopped moving. He was sober and alert. His voice was strong and clear.

We had just passed the road sign for Hartford. It was less than ten miles away. I checked the rearview mirror again but he was no longer talking. I drove slowly, watching the ditches. Where you find one deer, you will always find more I remembered. I had averted disaster once, next time I might not be so lucky.

The snow seemed to be deeper along the ditches. The southwestern corner of the state had been hit particularly hard by the winter storm. Ahead was another green road sign. This time Hartford was only three miles away.

"You better slow down, there's something going on up here."

I could see several cars on either side of the highway. Red and blue lights spun on their roofs. I counted three police cars. I slowed the truck to a gentle stop. A sheriff's deputy stood in the middle of the road with his right hand in front of him and his palm open. His fingers were extended inside of a black leather glove. He walked to my side of the pickup and made a circular motion while holding his index finger and thumb together, police sign language for roll down your window.

"Where are you folks headed?"

The deputy was stooped over slightly with his face centered in the window frame. Dad leaned to his left toward the opened window.

"We're on our way to Cedar Springs sir."

"The roads aren't too good yet. What's so urgent that you need to be out in this weather?"

"That's just it officer, my parents are up there alone in their farmhouse. They're elderly and I'm a little worried. I just want to make sure that they are okay. I tried calling but the phone lines must be down because the call wouldn't go through."

The deputy's eyes were inspecting every inch of the pickup cab as my father spoke. He was listening to what my father said but he was more interested in what was inside of our truck.

"What have you got under that blanket?"

"Just a pair of tired and cold legs, this is an old pickup, it's a miracle the heater works at all."

The deputy's eyes moved to the area behind the bench seat.

"And you're bringing your guns with you too."

I had forgotten about the shotguns sitting in the cases behind the seat of the truck. My heart started to race and my face felt suddenly warm.

"I hate to drive all the way up there without doing a little pheasant hunting. Cedar Springs has got a lot of birds this year."

The deputy stepped to the front of the pickup and wrote down our license plate number on a small notepad. He stepped back to the driver's door window.

"Have you got your license with you son?"

I slowly put my hand back in my pocket and pulled out my new plastic driver's license. My hand was shaking as I handed it to him.

"Tommy."

Nervously I responded, "Yes sir."

"We're looking for a young girl, nineteen years old. She's about five foot three, blonde hair and wearing a gray sweatshirt and a navy blue ski jacket. That's her car over there in the ditch. It looks like she spun out and then left her car after it skidded off the road. We're asking everyone to keep their eyes open for her. It's too cold out here to be trying to walk for help."

"Yes sir."

He handed me my license back and I put it back into my front pocket.

"Keep it slow. The roads are still slick."

I put the truck back into first gear. My legs felt like rubber. I was nervous and trembling. As I tried to let the clutch out my leg gave way and the truck shook hard nearly stalling. I quickly grabbed second gear

163

making the truck fishtail a bit. The deputy held out his hands as if to say, take it easy.

"Relax Tommy. No one knows what we're doing out here except you and me."

Dad was calm but I had broken into a sweat despite the freezing temperature. In the side mirror, I saw the deputy walk to the side of his fellow officer.

"What's their story?"

The deputy tucked the notepad back into his coat pocket.

"Just some kid and his dad worried about their grandparents up in Cedar Springs."

Chapter 24

As we moved further away from Hartford, the effects of the blizzard were fading quickly. The storm left a varied amount of snow across the state. Towns fifty miles apart had much different measurements of snowfall. Only a little snow had fallen across the middle of the state while the storm punished the northern towns with mammoth drifts and frozen roads. The southern half of the state had received a freezing rain, heavy snow and strong gusty winds that led to ground blizzards, which are blinding to someone trying to drive through them.

The part of the state where we were driving no longer had branches falling limp under the weight of the premature and wet snowfall. There were no sculpted drifts, just a gentle blanket of white spread evenly over the terrain. The maple trees still held some of their foliage. The bright orange and red treetops were a stark contrast to the white pastures.

The roads were no longer snow packed and icy. The blacktop was now dry.

Dad was alert. He was able to take in the scenery, to absorb its beauty. He surveyed the all too familiar landscape smiling occasionally, smiles fueled by some innate objects that had awoken some memories. I took exceptional pleasure in each smile.

I looked at my wristwatch. It was almost two o'clock.

"You're going to turn right on Highway 16."

Dad knew every paved and unpaved road in this part of the state. It had hardly changed since he was a young man. We were headed for the hillcrest grove, a set of trees that had long been a favorite hunting ground for my dad. It would be a killing field for a different reason today. We would make one final walk together, side-by-side, hunting for pheasants and then we would find a gentle place to release dad's soul.

The trees were in my sightline now. They were thick and tall and stretched nearly the entire fence line. They were surrounded on either side of a dried out creek bed. There was a driveway that crossed into an adjacent cornfield where the pheasants scavenged whatever food they could find. I brought the truck to a nice gentle stop on the approach to the field. We sat inside the truck surveying the remnants of the summer's corn harvest. We were sitting inside of a living oil painting. I admired its golden colors, its subtle hills and seemingly endless horizon was beautiful. I became lost in the moment. For a fleeting moment I forgot what this day truly represented; death and darkness, a new era in my life but mostly a sense of loneliness like I had never experienced before in my short life.

It was a peaceful site; the soft blue sky, the occasional red winged blackbird darting across the sky, the monstrous pine trees and the gentle rolling hills.

This was what I envisioned when dad set my Browning twenty gauge on the fender of his truck that first day of summer break. This was the pretty part, the anticipated part. What I had not foreseen at that time was our real purpose for being there. The ugliness of this moment would have never entered my thoughts with the promise of a summer break barely underway. That was of course before dad had become sick and mom had become someone that I no longer knew.

Our first hunting trip together was supposed to be fun, thrilling and filled with memories that would last me a lifetime. Now it would be fulfilling only one of those promises, in the form of a dark, morbid and morose memory. It would be the kind of memory that people spend years trying to undo by sitting on couches and telling their innermost feelings to strangers that call themselves psychiatrists.

I had to remind myself that this was dad's choice. I would rather have him at his parent's house surrounded by the sounds of the wild and the brilliant colors of fall rather than in some hospital bed surrounded by white walls, a cold tile floor and stainless steel medical equipment.

To me there was no question how a beautiful life should end; it should end in comfort, joy and in a place where your greatest memories are still alive.

That is where we were heading. That is what made this moment bearable. The feelings I would experience after this day were irrelevant right now. Today wasn't about my feelings five years from now; it was about my father and a peaceful ending to his life. It was about the man who gave me life and then sacrificed for the next fourteen years as he tried to bring me happiness.

It was soothing sitting there. A gentle breeze moved the tops of the trees just enough so that the different colors of the leaves melted into one another. The pines themselves swayed gently back and forth.

Dad rolled down his window, reached into his pocket and pulled out a familiar maroon box of Pall Mall cigarettes. He put a fresh white cigarette between his chapped lips and returned the pack to his shirt pocket. He opened the glove box and pulled a small box of wooden matchsticks. He struck the red and white head of the match against the side of the box igniting it and then held it to the tip of his cigarette.

He coughed but was undeterred. We sat there quietly captivated. I was afraid to break the silence and interrupt whatever thoughts were spinning through his mind.

"It's pretty, isn't it? I remember coming out here when I was your age. Your Grandpa and I would sit right here in his pickup."

Dad began one of his coughing spells. He held his cigarette out the door window with his right hand while he coughed into a handkerchief that he held with his left.

"I was wrong for so many years thinking that it was the farm that killed him; all of those fourteen hour days, the droughts and the thunderstorms that seem to come out of nowhere. It seemed like he could never catch his breath."

Dad took a long drag off his cigarette and scratched his ear with his left hand.

"Just because he died working here doesn't mean that the farm killed him. Here I have been casting the blame in the wrong direction for years now. The farm didn't kill him. The farm gave him life. All of that hard work and those long days gave him a purpose. That's why he got up before the sun broke the horizon and that's why he didn't come home until it had started to set again. He did what he did out of a love for this land. He loved feeling connected to the dirt and the trees. They were like children to him. He was their caretaker. Uncle Tommy wasn't the only one who died doing what he loved, grandpa did too. He would have fallen ill with cancer whether he was driving a combine or selling stocks on Wall Street."

Dad stretched his legs and threw his cigarette butt out of the truck window.

"You can't truly control your own destiny Tommy, at least not every part of it."

My father's appearance had changed since we had left our house. He was vibrant. He was sitting straighter and his eyes were keener. He was more alive than I had seen him in days.

"Tommy, do what makes you happy. Let life take you wherever it takes you. It's just a giant amusement park ride anyway. Don't let time leave you with any regrets. When I'm gone, you'll still have all the memories of us. Those memories won't ever die."

It was a lot for a fourteen year old to think about, especially when I knew my purpose for being there today. I didn't want my father dying and leaving any regrets. I wanted to reassure him that I understood. I wanted to tell him something that would let him know how important he was to me and so many other people.

"Dad, maybe God put you here as a teacher?"

Dad looked at me and was listening intently. I think he was in agreement. His with his mouth closed and his eyes were intense.

"Think of all of the things that you have taught me and all of the people that you have influenced. They all respect you and look up to you."

My words seemed to be providing him with a sense of comfort and fulfillment. I don't know what prompted me to say what I said at that moment but it seemed to have been the perfect choice of words.

"You know what Tommy. I think you may be right."

We sat there a moment longer as dad took in the brilliance of the landscape. My heart was heavy but today wasn't about me. Today was about dad and his transition from mortal man to spirit world.

Dad reached over and placed his once formidable hand on my wrist.

"It's time", he said softly.

They were two simple words but two words that carried a complex and profound meaning. I simply nodded okay and with guns in hand; we began the short walk to the groves, which would forever be my father's final resting place.

Chapter 25

It was about a difficult walk through the frozen furrows of the cornfields. In his weakened state dad was doing well to navigate the uneven terrain. My palms were sweaty and I felt tightness in my chest that seemed to squeeze a little harder with each passing moment. When doubts entered into my head, I reminded myself of the conversation that we had on the porch of our house. I had my chance to say no to his request at that time. I could have said no and dad would have loved me just the same but I had remained silent.

The brush ahead of us suddenly started moving. A frenzied flapping of wings ensued as two pheasants, both of them roosters, took flight. On any other day, they would have been our dinner but we weren't there to collect roosters.

I watched as the roosters took flight some twenty yards in front of us. I never noticed before what beautiful birds they were with their brightly colored feathers. They flew so effortlessly toward the grove of trees and disappeared into the backdrop of the pines and the uncut wild grass.

Dad plodded along and I paced myself to stay shoulder to shoulder with him. I could tell by the expression on his face that each step in the frozen dirt sent shivers of pain through his muscles and joints. He was also laboring and struggling to catch his breath but his determination and willpower kept him moving forward.

His shotgun was tipped with the barrel pointed skyward and was leaning against his right shoulder. There was a strange symbolism in a biblical sense. Jesus had carried his cross to his own crucifixion and now my father carried his shotgun to what he knew would be his final resting place.

The trees were drawing closer and so was my apprehension. Just when I thought my heart couldn't beat any faster it found a way. I had never felt quite like this before in my life. There was an enormous amount of pressure growing inside of my head. My eardrums felt like they could explode at any moment. I could feel my pulse pounding in the temple on the side of my head. My throat was sore from breathing in the cold autumn air. I was locked into a living nightmare but unlike the dreams that had found their way into my sleep this was a nightmare that I couldn't wake myself up from. I knew how this dream was going to end. The conclusion was now only a short distance ahead of us.

Dad stopped at a small plateau and bent forward over his knees breathing heavily. More roosters raced out from under the brush ahead of us. This time they stayed on the ground and disappeared out of sight. The pine trees stood behind my father like a giant Hollywood backdrop. They stretched for hundreds of feet from side to side. They were mammoth compared to us.

Dad straightened his back and took a series of shallow breaths. We stared at each other silently. I was in no condition to speak. I was paralyzed in fear and I could barely breathe at this point myself. Dad was calm and in a state of relief that could be mistaken for excitement that his suffering was about to end.

"This is it. This is the place."

I nodded unenthusiastically.

"Daddy's waiting. Mom is waiting. Tommy is waiting. They're all waiting for me son."

"I know dad."

"It's the right thing Tommy. I mean look at me. You're just sending me to a better place a little bit early. You're freeing my spirit from this broken down old shell of a body. It's going to be okay."

No matter how hard I tried this time I couldn't squeeze my eyes hard enough to hold back my tears. The reality of the moment had finally overwhelmed me.

Dad walked over and wrapped his arms around my shoulders. Even with the weight he had lost, he still dwarfed my fourteen-year old body. Even with the strength he had lost, he still hugged me as tightly as he always had. And even with death's shadow being cast down upon us from the giant evergreen trees, he was still as brave as ever.

"I love you Tommy."

"I love you too, Dad."

"Remember what I said, I'm always just a short prayer away."

I knew what he was telling me was intended to give me comfort but a prayer couldn't wrap its arms around me the same way that my father could and a prayer couldn't cast a fishing line. His words gave me comfort but there is only so much comfort that can be gained from a dying father's words.

"Just do the right thing Tommy. Choose the right path and life will take you as far as you let it take you."

"Dad I'm going to pray to you every night and someday we'll be together again just like you and your father right?"

I grabbed a hold of dad and hugged him again one final time. The tears streamed down my cheeks faster and more furious than ever. I knew that this was it. This was our last hug, our last words, and our one final minute on Earth together.

Dad stepped back about fifteen feet from me and laid his gun in the field. I used the arm of my coat to wipe the tears from my eyes. I gave my shotgun a quick pump loading the shell into the chamber. My legs began to tremble underneath of me making it difficult for me to steady the shotgun. I took two deep breaths and exhaled each of them slowly trying to calm my nerves.

Dad stood with his chest facing me. He had just enough of a smile to make the corners of his mouth pull upward.

I leveled my shotgun at him. It had to be just one shot to be an accident so my aim had to be perfect. I had struggled at times shooting the clay pigeons but they were in motion and flying through the air. My father was stationary. I placed the front sight of the gun's barrel on the center of his chest. If I fired now the shrapnel would rip through his chest and tear his heart into pieces. That would be the surest way to inflict a mortal wound. The choke on my shotgun had been adjusted so that the pellets would be propelled in a small and tight formation.

My hands were moist with perspiration and slipped as I slid the safety of my gun to the off position.

"I love you, Tommy", my father said in a soft and gentle voice.

My hands were trembling now. The shaking had moved from my legs into my arms. I had to move my hand away from the trigger again as I cleared my away the tears that were blurring my vision. Dad's chest was coming in and out of position on the sight of my gun.

"You can do it Tommy", he said as he tried to encourage me.

Twenty seconds passed as I attempted to try and steady my aim. It felt like I had leveled my shotgun at my father for an eternity already.

"Breathe Tommy, in and out just like I taught you at the firing range".

It wasn't just like he had taught me at the firing range. Those targets were lifeless discs of hard clay. They had no families or feelings. They were emotionless inanimate objects. A shot through a clay pigeon had no effect on any other living being.

I lowered the gun to my waist and my father lowered his arms to his side. We both needed a moment to gather our strength. I breathed again trying to regain my composure but my hands were still trembling and my legs felt like they were made out of jelly.

"Be a man", I said to myself in a scolding voice. I had to be a man. We had come too far for me to fail my father now. We had planned this out right down to the story that I would relay to anyone who questioned what had happened. I couldn't disappoint him, not now. Not after all that he had done for me in my life.

I took control of my breathing just as my father had instructed me. I raised my arms and placed the stock of the gun back against my right shoulder. My arms came to a relaxed and controlled position. My legs were planted firmly under my hips. I had good balance and finally I had control of the gun. It was steady and I had the bead of the barrel directly over his heart. Dad held his arms out to his side again, ready to be released from the pain that had gained such a stronghold in the last few weeks. With one squeeze of the trigger, he would instantly be with God. He would know the answer to one of the greatest unanswered questions known to man, what comes after death.

I squeezed my finger toward me, slowly and gently. There was a thunderous echo as the gunpowder in the shell exploded. A hundred blackbirds were scared from the tops of the pine trees and joined together in a giant black cluster that moved gently over the top of me in the sky. I dropped the shotgun on the soil beside me and sat down in a pile of flesh, crying hysterically. My body shook forward with each sob. How could I have done this to my father, the man who would do anything for me?

The wind gusted and small pellets of frozen rain began to batter against the side of my face. My head was buried in my hands. I felt more alone then I ever had before.

Suddenly two gloved hands came to rest on my shoulders.

"Tommy, it's okay."

"I can't do it dad. I don't want to let you down but I just can't do it."

I continued to weep and my father dropped down to his knees and wrapped his arms around me one more time.

My father, the man who was dying from cancer comforted me because I couldn't fulfill his one dying wish. That's the kind of man he was though. He wasn't mad at me and if he was disappointed I couldn't tell. The only thing he cared about was how I was feeling at that moment. It was the same selflessness that he had exhibited to me my whole life.

"I had the gun aimed. I had it in line for a kill shot but I couldn't do it. I couldn't let that be the last my last memory of you. I've got all of these great memories of us and that one would have spoiled them all."

My heartbeat slowed and I wiped palms on the legs of my pants. The chill of the air made its way through my winter jacket and the small pellets of sleet continued to batter us as we sat alone together in the field.

"Come on", he said as he stood up and helped me back to my feet. He draped his arm around my neck for support and we made our way back across the ruddy field to the pickup. The walk had physically taken a toll on my father and now he was using me as his human crutch. We were both drained, me emotionally and he physically.

"It's going to be okay, Tommy. You did the right thing. I was the one who told you as long as you make decisions by using your heart, you'll never disappoint me."

Inside of myself I felt like I had disappointed him. We had driven ninety miles through less than desirable weather in order to keep my father from dying inside the lonely walls of a hospital. In my mind I had failed him. We hobbled across the field as we were peppered by the frozen rain until we finally reached the pickup.

"Let's drive out to the farmhouse. We came this far, it's only a couple of miles away."

Chapter 26

It was a short ride from the grove to the farmhouse. I turned onto the weed ridden driveway and parked the truck. It would be a short walk this time and since dad was already physically exhausted, that was important.

My father folded the quilt, which had been wrapped around his legs and placed a bible on top of it that he had intended on reading while we were making the drive. The bible had gone unopened since he had slept for most of the trip to Cedar Springs.

Dad stepped out of the truck first holding the quilt, his bible and his shotgun. I followed him as he made his way up onto the old wooden porch. The snow that was on the ground kicked loosely in front of his boots. He pulled open the rotting front door and moved into what had once been the living room.

Dad laid the quilt down on the floor in front of the old brick fireplace and leaned his shotgun against the wall. He unfolded it and spread it out and laid the bible at one corner of it.

"There's a pile of firewood that Earl keeps behind the house. Go get an armful and bring it on in so we can get some heat in here."

I walked out to the side of the house. Several of the old trees that had died on the property had already been cut down and chopped into kindling wood. I picked up as much as I could fit into my arms and returned to the living room.

Dad neatly stacked a few of the logs in the fireplace. He took a box of stick matches from his pocket and looked around in search of something to use as an accelerant to start the fire.

"Tommy, in the glove box in the truck there are a few road maps. Go and get them."

I ran outside to the pickup again. There inside of the glove box were three Rand McNally roadmaps. I grabbed them and pushed against the wind, which was gaining strength and walked back into the house to where my father was. He was sitting on the quilt now. He took the maps from me and quickly rolled one up into a tight round wad. He struck the wooden match to the side of the box and held the flame to the corner of the map. The paper ignited and he tucked the map underneath the kindling that he had placed inside of the fireplace.

"Not bad for a couple of amateurs", dad said with a smile of relief. He blew gently on the small flame and soon a corner of a log had caught fire. The logs were cold but the wood was extremely dry. My uncle had chopped that kindling months ago so the wood had been sitting for long enough to dry out.

Dad took a second map and positioned it as a bridge of sorts to carry the flame that started on the bottom log to the large piece of kindling that was lying on the top. The map burst into fire as large flames licked at the wood. Small black pieces of burned map floated in the air and fell harmlessly to the bottom of the fireplace.

The logs slowly caught fire and heat began to emanate from the front of the fireplace. The logs crackled and popped as the flames that engulfed them grew taller and more intense.

"Tommy, do me a favor and go get another armful of the firewood and bring it in. I want to put it near the fireplace so it'll be ready if I need it."

I ran back out around the house and filled my arms again with as much kindling as I could carry. I brought them in and sat them on the side of the fireplace where they could be warmed.

The flames inside of the fireplace were thriving now. Dad was sitting a couple feet away from the fire on the quilt. He was moving his hands over one another trying to restore some warmth and circulation to his fingertips.

I sat down beside him on the quilt and leaned inward to share what little body heat the two of us were producing. I had a chill running through me as well.

"We used to roast marshmallows in here when dad would let us. Your uncle ruined that when he caught the curtains on fire that hung over that window. Earl decided it would be a good idea to chase Art while he had a flaming marshmallow on a stick. Of course Art tripped and fell right into that damn curtain. Needless to say, that was the end of our indoor campfires."

The fireplace was growing warmer. It became more and more comfortable in front of the fireplace.

"I'm going to stay here. Do you know your way to Aunt Gloria's house from here?"

"Three left turns?"

"That's right. It's simple. When you get to a road where you can only go right or left, turn to the left. Do that three times and you'll be there before you know it."

Dad looked at me soberly.

"You didn't disappoint me Tommy. This is actually better. I'm home. This is where my life started. I've come full circle now. I'll be okay."

Dad broke into a major coughing spell that lasted for over a minute. I waited patiently until it ended.

"Everything else in the house might be falling apart but the fireplace still works."

Dad put another piece of firewood on the flames that were now roaring inside of the stone fireplace.

"I should've brought some marshmallows huh?"

I said nothing but forced a small smile.

"The police are going to ask you why you left me here."

"Because you asked me to and you're my father. Isn't that a good enough reason?"

Dad pulled out a cigarette and lit it. He could barely take a drag from the end of it before he would start coughing. He took the white handkerchief back out of his pocket and held it over his mouth. It's going to sound strange but it was comforting to see the blood left behind on the handkerchief from his coughing spells. It reaffirmed what I already knew, my dad was enduring unnecessary pain.

"When you wake up tomorrow your life is going to be different in a lot of ways, but that's how life us all of the time."

Dad pointed toward the room that I had visited my grandmother in on many a night before she passed away.

"Just think I was born right inside of there, through that door and on that same old iron bed frame. Back when I was little a lot of us were born right where we lived. They didn't have big wings in hospitals dedicated to women waiting to have babies."

Grandma's bedroom was in a direct line with our vision from where we sat on the quilt.

I didn't know how long I could hold my composure but I didn't want to leave dad's side either. I had a hunch that he was feeling the same way as I was.

He only finished half of the cigarette and then threw it into the fireplace.

"I can't even taste those stupid things anymore. There's no point in smoking them if you can't taste them."

I knew the time had come for me to leave his side. If I waited any longer, I wouldn't want to go. I had bought a little extra time with him. I got the idea that every second I stuck around it was getting harder and harder for my dad to let me loose also.

"I'll walk you out to the truck to make sure it starts up, okay? It's too cold to be out there walking around if you slide off of the road or the thing stops running so if you run into any trouble just stay inside and wait for somebody to stop and help you."

Dad stood up and I followed his lead. He put his hand on my shoulder as we walked. He wasn't supporting his weight; he was making a connection with me and providing me with comfort. He followed me down the steps to the side of the truck. As soon as we were there, I turned and hugged him as tightly as I could. He rubbed my shoulders comforting me. I held on to him firmly not wanting to let go. I wanted to say something to let him know that I was strong. I spoke with my mouth pressed into his shoulder as we hugged.

"I'll bring your ashes back out to the grove this spring to your favorite spot", I told him.

"You aren't going to need to Tommy. My ashes will already be here."

We stopped outside and looked at the house that had brought my father so many cheerful memories. It was beginning to tip toward the left and the roof was sagging even worse than it was when we came out here a few months earlier.

"I think there might be an accident here today after all."

Dad and I turned back around and made our way over to the truck. He pulled at the handle on the driver's side door and swung it open for me. It was my signal to get inside and move on to my Aunt Gloria's house.

I sat myself behind the steering wheel, closed the door and rolled down the window. The sleet had turned into light, fluffy white snowflakes. The wind had softened as well and no longer blew with the ferocity and coldness that it had only a short time earlier.

"Until we meet again", my father said with a reassuring smile.

"Until we meet again", I echoed."

Dad leaned his head in through the window frame and gave me a single kiss on my forehead. He pulled his head back out and gave me a wink. I watched him as he took a few steps backward away from the truck making room for me to steer it in a circle so I could drive out.

I turned the key starting the engine and carefully turned the pickup around in the driveway. I adjusted the rearview mirror so I could see behind me. Dad was standing several feet back and squarely behind the tailgate.

I flashed back to that moment at the beginning of the summer when he had laid that shotgun out on the fender of his truck for me. Back then I thought that receiving the gun as a gift and turning fourteen were the rites of passage into manhood. Now life had offered me a new perspective, one that I wished no other child would ever have to experience.

I learned that becoming a man was about standing strong in the face of adversity. It wasn't about a physical age barrier; it was about a mental strength barrier. I was taking my final strides toward manhood right now. I was being forced to become a man because soon I would no longer have a father to lean on for my strength.

The low idling sound of the exhaust and the whirling sound of the country wind blended into a lonely winter chorus on the driveway of the abandoned farmhouse.

"I'm going to make you proud", I said out loud to myself inside the cab of the pickup.

The power of those six words was immense. I knew that if I made him proud that it would mean that I have always made the right decisions. That would it would mean that I had done the right thing because I knew what he stood for. To make him proud I would have to abide by the values he had instilled in me. If I did that I would ensure that I was staying on the right path.

I stuck my hand out of the window and waved to him. He stood bravely under the blanket of lightly falling snow and waved back. I wanted to leave a strong impression. I refused to let him see me cry again.

I drove the truck down the driveway to the gravel road that led away from the house. The giant trees and the old farmhouse were framed behind him like a Norman Rockwell painting. I had to make two more left turns before I would find my way to my aunt's house. I pressed my foot down on the clutch and gently moved the truck into second gear.

My father was a man who had always been larger than life to me and now he was dwarfed by the giant pine trees that surrounded him. His image became smaller and smaller until it was nothing more than a dark colored dot with no distinguishable characteristics.

I never heard the concussion of a fatal gunshot but I have felt its imagined reverberation what seems like a hundred times. It has awoken me in the dead of the night with my body jolted from a sound sleep.

On a few nights in the months that have passed I have found myself in a dream where I am driving dad's truck recklessly through the back roads of South Dakota. I am steering it with my left hand while I wipe away an endless flow of tears with my right hand.

I am in a cold sweat and trembling with my hands clenched tightly around the steering wheel. The unmistakable smell of gunpowder fills the cab of the pickup. The odor is stuck in my nasal cavity and I am unable to flush it from my nose.

I continue to drive down a narrow gravel road until I am met by a parade of fire engines speeding in the direction of where I just came from. Behind me in the mirror I see a billowing cloud of smoke that seems to stretch all the way to the heavens.

As the final fire engine passes me on the highway I find myself sitting on the side of the road in the idling truck.

I want to turn the truck around but I can't. The steering wheel is stuck and I can't turn it to the left or to the right. I desperately want to drive back for one glimpse of my superhero and for one final reassuring smile that will tell me that things will be okay but I cannot. We had exchanged our final glance already.

That dream has played identically for me several times. I find it is eerily similar to what happened on that chilly fall day. It ends with one single thunderous gunshot exploding in the air as I sit in the truck on the side of the road.

November 5th, 1983 brought an end my father's pain and an end to a summer that I will never forget. It was and will always be the summer that I became, the cold November son.

The End

Made in the USA
Charleston, SC
06 January 2011